Read all the books about Madison Finn!

Coming Soon!

Don't miss the Super Edition

From the Files of

Madison Finn

Give Me a Break

By Laura Dower

HYPERION
New York

Text copyright © 2004 by Laura Dower

From the Files of Madison Finn and the Volo colophon are trademarks of Disney Enterprises, Inc.
Volo® is a registered trademark of Disney Enterprises, Inc.

Printed in the United States of America

First Edition
3 5 7 9 10 8 6 4 2

The main body of text of this book is set in 13-point Frutiger Roman.

ISBN 0-7868-0988-4

Visit www.hyperionbooksforchildren.com

For
Rich, Myles,
and Olivia

Special thanks
to the wonderful Louise
for everything she does

Chapter 1

"Ready, aim, *fire!*"

Madison jumped out of the way just in time to see a snowball go whizzing past her earmuffs. It hit one of Madison's BFFs, Fiona Waters, instead of her.

"Ooof!" Fiona cried, pretending to be wounded. She collapsed onto the snowy ground, hands on her chest, laughing.

"Good one!" Chet Waters said, giving Walter "Egg" Diaz a high five. Chet was Fiona's twin brother. All afternoon he'd been aiming for his sister, but Egg was the one who had finally struck the target.

"I can't believe it was you who threw it!" Fiona said as she stood up and brushed the snow off her grape-colored corduroys.

Aimee Gillespie laughed, too. "Maybe Egg doesn't like you so much after all."

Splooooch!

Another one of Egg's snowballs scored a direct hit, on Aimee this time. The entire front of her parka was soaked.

Chet doubled over with laughter. If this was a snowball match of guys versus girls, there was no question who was winning. So far.

"You'd better run! You're in trouble, Egg," Hart Jones said to his friend. He shoved his hands into his pockets. "Aimee's going get you for—"

Splaaaat!

Hart groaned. Now he'd been hit in the face with a very cold ball of snow. He wiped off his chin and turned around to see who had thrown it.

Madison jumped into the air with glee. "Gotcha, Hart!" she said with a big grin. She pumped her arm as if to show off a muscle, which of course was invisible underneath her winter coat. "Maybe I should try out for the softball team?" she asked, still giggling.

Hart leaned over and picked up a fistful of snow. "Don't move," he warned Madison, pulling his arm back like a major-league pitcher.

That was when snowball chaos broke out.

Hart threw another snowball at Madison, who ran for cover behind a tree. Chet fired three snowballs in a row at his sister, narrowly missing her each time. Egg wasn't even making snowballs anymore.

He just chucked clumps of snow wherever he could, including the side of the house. Fiona and Aimee tried running away, but they tripped over themselves in the snow and fell to the ground, laughing uncontrollably.

The six friends had come over to Aimee's backyard after school to hang out. Winter break was coming soon, and no one felt much like doing homework or taking school seriously.

"Hot chocolate!" Mrs. Gillespie called out from the kitchen door.

Aimee threw her arms into the air. "Truce!" she said, so that everyone would stop the snowball fight. "Hot cocoa!"

The friends shuffled through the snow and ice toward the house. They peeled off layers of wet clothes and their jackets, gloves, and socks inside the back entryway. Then they all planted themselves somewhere on one of the two huge, tattered sofas in Aimee's basement—boys on one sofa, girls on the other. Mrs. Gillespie brought down cups of steaming hot chocolate.

"Your cheeks are so red," Hart said to Madison.

Naturally, she felt them get even redder when he pointed that out. But they weren't hot; they felt like ice cubes.

"Hey, this is even better than Mom's special recipe," Chet said to Fiona as he took another sip of hot chocolate.

Fiona blew on hers. "You're right," she said to her brother. "Thanks for having us over, Aim. This is a great time. I love snowy days like this."

Egg stood up and surveyed the bookshelves in the Gillespie basement. "What are all these?" he said, pointing to a large collection of record albums against one wall.

Aimee shrugged. "My dad collected those. He has this huge collection of eighties music. He says they're worth something. But I don't see the point. We can't even play them anymore."

Egg lifted up a few album covers. On one record was a photo of some odd-looking band members with red plastic plant pots upside down on their heads. The band was called Devo. Another album was called *Tears for Fears*. "He listens to *this*?" Egg asked. "What kind of a band name is A Flock of Seagulls?"

"When are you guys leaving for California?" Hart asked Fiona and Chet. Before living in Far Hills, Fiona and Chet's family had lived in California. They were flying back that week for a family visit.

"We're leaving after the big hockey match," Fiona said. "When is that again?"

"You forgot already? I told you it's on Sunday," Chet said to Fiona.

"Gee, I'm sorry!" Fiona cracked. "What? Do you expect me to remember everything?"

"Yeah!" Egg said. He and Fiona had been "going out" for a little while, but sometimes they talked

4

to each other as if they'd been together forever.

"Is next week's hockey match really all that important?" Aimee asked.

Hart clutched his chest as if she'd just shot him with a dart. "Are you kidding me?" he said.

Egg gasped, too. "Yeah! Are you kidding us?"

"All hockey games are important, Aim," Chet said. "Not that you, Maddie, or my sister would ever show up to watch us play."

"Good one!" Egg said. The three boys laughed.

The truth was that Aimee, Madison, and Fiona *had* gone to a few hockey games—and practices, too. Fiona went because her brother was on the team and because she wanted to see Egg in slap-shot action. Madison went to ogle Hart in his ice skates. And Aimee went whenever she didn't have dance practice, because Fiona and Madison were there.

"Actually," Hart said. "Since we all have our skates with us, maybe we should head over to the lake and practice a little."

"That's a killer idea!" Egg said, jumping up from the couch. "Let's go."

"Let's go," Chet repeated, putting down his now-empty mug.

"You guys, it's going to be dark in a half hour," Fiona said. "Chet, Mom will kill you if you're over at the lake when it gets too late."

Chet shrugged. "She won't *kill* me. She'll yell. Whatever."

Fiona rolled her eyes. "I am not sticking up for you."

"Like he cares," Egg said.

Fiona crossed her arms and pouted at Egg. The boys collected their semidry coats from Mrs. Gillespie, booted up, and headed out the back door again.

"See you tomorrow, 'kay?" Egg said to Fiona.

She managed a small smile. "Fine," she whispered.

After the boys had left, Madison collapsed back onto one of the sofas with a sigh.

"I have an announcement to make," Madison said. "This is going to be the most boring winter break in the history of the world."

"Why?" Fiona asked.

"I don't want to hang out in Far Hills doing nothing but watch *them* play hockey," Madison complained.

Aimee nodded. "I wish I were going somewhere exciting, like you, Fiona," she said. "You're so lucky to go back to California on school vacations. Sun, surf, cute skater boys . . ."

"Yeah," Fiona said. "But *you* try flying across the country sitting next to my brother!"

Aimee and Madison chuckled.

"I just wish I didn't have to work at my dad's bookstore," Aimee said. "He makes me shelve books *for hours*. And after that I have to clear tables in the

Cyber Cafe. Isn't there some kind of child-labor law about that?"

"I thought you liked working at the store," Fiona said.

"I did when it was the Christmas rush. But that's because Ben Buckley kept coming in to see me," Aimee said with a grin. "He must have brought me fifteen candy canes. That was so nice."

Ben was Aimee's seventh-grade super crush and the smartest guy in their class, hands down.

Aimee stood up from the sofa. "What are we sitting around down here for? Let's go up to my room. Mom just got me this all-natural makeup kit she saw in a health-food store. It smells nice. Let's give each other minimakeovers."

"Healthy makeup? What is it made from—tofu?" Fiona giggled. "Your mom is a health nut, Aim."

"You're just figuring this out?" Madison said.

They made a pit stop in the kitchen on the way up to Aimee's room, placed their empty cocoa mugs in the sink, and grabbed a bag of whole-wheat pretzels.

Aimee's room was a disaster zone. Pink ballet gear had been thrown into every corner of the room. A pair of toe shoes was hanging from the dresser knobs. Across her bed were a few well-worn copies of *En Pointe*, a ballet magazine she'd borrowed from the studio where she took lessons.

"What's *this*?" Madison asked. She held up a

letter printed on bright yellow paper that she'd found on the floor.

"Oh, you can throw that out," Aimee said. "It's just a dumb chain letter someone in my ballet class gave to me."

"What?" Madison exclaimed. "There is no such thing as a dumb chain letter."

Fiona giggled. "Maddie, you're the most superstitious person I know."

"Just toss the letter in the trash, Maddie," Aimee said again.

Madison clutched the letter to her chest. "Aimee, did you even read what this says? It says here that if you don't send this letter to five other people, then you will have five years of bad luck. You don't want five *years* of bad luck, do you? That would mean you'd have bad luck through your entire years of junior high and high school."

"Oh, Maddie," Aimee scoffed. "Give me a break. I don't believe in bad luck. That's just some kind of scam."

Madison wouldn't give the letter back to Aimee. "We have to send it to someone."

"I know what we could do," Fiona said. "Let's leave a copy in Ivy Daly's locker."

The three BFFs laughed and crouched down on the floor together, sitting knee to knee. Ivy was their number-one enemy. They called her Poison Ivy. The way Fiona figured it, if there was bad luck to be had . . . why not give it to the enemy?

"That's perfect!" Madison said. "Maybe passing Ivy the letter means she will get cursed, and then she'll get five years of bad luck."

"Yeah," Aimee said. "And then she'll stop muscling in on Hart."

"What are you talking about?" Madison said.

"Hart," Fiona said. "Your Hart."

"Well, I don't know about Hart these days. . . ." Madison said, her voice trailing off.

"What?" Aimee said. "Are we talking about the same Hart who you were just flirting with in my yard and my house?"

"I was not flirting," Madison said.

"You're such a liar!" Fiona and Aimee both cried at the same time.

"I'm not lying," Madison said. "Can't I change my mind? It's winter break, right? Maybe it's time I took a break from him. Maybe I should find a new crush."

"Are you feeling okay?" Aimee asked, a little more seriously. She actually sounded concerned. "I thought you really, *really* liked Hart. Don't you?"

"I guess I like him," Madison replied. "When he isn't acting like a boy."

The trio burst into laughter.

"Well, Maddie," Fiona said, "If you really don't like Hart anymore, then you'd better be careful, because he might go out with Ivy after all. . . ."

"Bite your tongue!" Madison said.

"Maybe it's a good thing," Aimee continued. "It's spring break. Maddie can find some new guys to crush on."

"In Far Hills?" Madison said, sounding not very enthusiastic about her prospects.

They lay back on the floor and flipped through some of the books and magazines around the room, talking more about crushes and boys and about how slow everything felt in the middle of winter. Aimee showed off her new, all-natural makeup set, and they took turns putting eye shadow and eyeliner on one another. The all-natural stuff didn't come in any shades other than brown and browner (no hot pinks or neon oranges in this set), but it was still fun to do makeovers. It always was.

After it got dark outside, Mrs. Gillespie came up to Aimee's room and asked the girls to stay for dinner. But Fiona and Madison both decided to head home instead. Fiona had to get home to pack for her cross-country trip, and Madison wanted to spend a little time with her mom and her pug, Phinnie.

On the short walk up Blueberry Street to her house, Madison thought more about her crush on Hart. She realized that it wasn't exactly *fading*, but it was getting a little stuck. Neither she nor Hart seemed willing to put themselves out there and really find out whether the other person was "in like." Through friends they had learned some key information. They'd discovered that they had some things in common. They had even shared a bucket of popcorn at a group movie date. But that was it.

Wasn't there something more? Was this how it worked with all boys?

Dinner was already on the table when Madison walked through the door. Her mom had made spaghetti with vegetarian nonmeatballs and some special marinara sauce that Gramma Helen had sent to them. Gramma always cooked and knit during the winter and sent Madison and Mom care packages.

As Madison helped set the table, Phinnie rubbed up against her ankles.

"There he goes again," Mom said. "Looking for a pug hug!"

Madison loved the way her dog always let her know what he needed. Why couldn't boys be the same?

After dinner, Madison carried Phin upstairs. She booted up her laptop and headed for her favorite Web site, bigfishbowl.com. She was hoping to chat with Fiona or Aimee, but neither of her friends was online. In fact, no one from Madison's buddy list, not even her cross-country keypal, Bigwheels, was online.

The next destination was Madison's files.

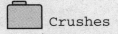 Crushes

    News flash: My friends think I am
bonkers, but I've decided to rethink the
whole Hart thing. It breaks my heart

(Hart?) to do this, because he is hands down the cutest guy (I think) in seventh grade. But I wonder if maybe it wasn't really meant to be between him and me. That would be my bad luck, wouldn't it?

My hugest crush was (and is) Jimmie J, the lead singer of my fave band, but there's no chance he'll ever even know who I am, unless I suddenly became a rock star and meet him on the red carpet somewhere. Hey, that could happen! 8:-P

There's that guy Toby next door. I wish he didn't have a gf. Then again, he's too old for me.

And then there's Mark. He wasn't really a crush. He was something else, something real (:>) But I totally BLEW IT with Mark. I never even e-mailed him after I got back from Gramma's house--and after I'd kissed him! On the lips! Actually, he never e-mailed me, either. At first I was super happy about knowing him because Mark is so nice and it was summer when we met and the fireworks were so romantic. So why did I wimp out? Maybe I was scared? I mean, he's the only boy I've ever kissed. That's a HUGE deal.

The truth is that inside I was a little sad. No matter what, I think I wanted HART to be the first everything, not some stranger named Mark.

Maybe I still do want Hart to be everything. Ugh. That sounds so sappy.

Madison glanced away from the laptop screen. It was hard to think that one of her biggest dreams—to be part of a couple with Hart—just couldn't seem to work. Madison hit the backspace key to erase the last part of her file entry. She had to stop writing about and start forgetting Hart.

Aimee was right. Right?

Winter break was a good time to crush on some new boys? Right?

"Maddie!" A voice yelled from downstairs. "Maddie! Pick up the phone! It's your dad!"

Madison jumped up from where she'd been sitting on her bed, stubbing her toe in the process. She limped to Mom's room and grabbed the phone.

"Dad?" Madison said. She heard Mom hang up the extension.

"Maddie," Dad wheezed. "I just got the best news, and I wanted to call you right away!" he said.

"Were you just running?" Madison asked. "You sound breathless."

"No, no!" Dad chuckled. "Maddie, I'm just excited! I am calling you about winter break. You still don't have any major plans, do you?"

"No . . ." Madison was intrigued.

"Well, pack your bags!" Dad exclaimed. "We're heading to Big Mountain!"

Madison's head started to spin as Dad explained. He'd gotten last-minute time off from work, and one of his clients had given him an incredible gift: a weeklong reservation for Treetops Lodge, one of the most exclusive lodges up on Big Mountain, which was a ski resort in the Adirondack Mountains. Stephanie, Dad's new wife, was taking time off from work, too; and they wanted Madison to join them. It meant packing and leaving for the trip at the crack of dawn on Saturday morning.

"Wow," Madison was speechless.

"That's not even the best part!" Dad cried. "Stephanie and I want you to bring Phin. This lodge has babysitting *and* dog-sitting."

"Really?" Madison said, still dumbfounded.

"And that's not all!" Dad said, sounding like a game-show host who was announcing the big-prize package. "We want you to bring a friend."

"A friend?" Madison squealed. "Really?"

Now her head was spinning. She'd only gone skiing once, and she'd never gone on vacation with a friend. This could be a lot of fun.

Without warning, Madison's winter break was beginning to morph into a very real escape—at one of the ritziest ski lodges around.

And Madison knew *exactly* whom she would invite.

Chapter 2

On Friday morning, Madison couldn't finish her cereal. Already her mind was up at the Big Mountain ski resort and Treetops Lodge.

There she was, sipping cocoa next to her own personal lodge fireplace, skating figure eights around a packed ice rink, snow-tubing with her BFF, and skiing down the slopes at breakneck speed.

And there was Phinnie, skiing on little doggy skis. Madison chuckled to herself.

"What's so funny?" Mom asked, rubbing sleep out of her eyes. She'd been up half the night working on a deadline for her latest project with Budge Films.

"I was just thinking. . . ." Madison said dreamily.

The doorbell rang.

"Aimee!" Madison screamed, and she dashed for the door.

When she opened it, Aimee stood there, biting her lip.

"Well, well . . ." Madison said. "What did your dad say? Can you come?"

Aimee kicked at the welcome mat. Then she looked Madison right in the eye.

"I can come!" she said, her mouth curling into a huge watermelon slice of a grin. "I can come!"

Madison and Aimee began jumping up and down quickly. Phin, who'd come to the front door to say hello, backed away from all the excitement.

Mom came out of the kitchen. "Off to school, you two," she said. "You need to face one more day of reality before the fun starts."

Madison kissed Mom on the cheek, grabbed her orange bag with her left hand and Aimee's hand with her right.

"We're going on a ski trip together!" Madison said over and over again, as if she were repeating some kind of mantra. "See you later, Far Hills!"

Aimee was talking so much she could hardly catch her breath. She said that the moment she had hung up the phone after Madison had called the night before to invite her, she had started packing.

"Dad said he could really use me at the store," Aimee said. "But then he winked and said he couldn't let me pass up a trip like this. He says Treetops is like one of those places where people go to be seen. And now *we* can see them! Wahoo! I packed my parka, my favorite jeans, my blue sweater—you know the one with the little snowman on it?"

"So you're cool about missing dance practice next week?" Madison asked. Aimee never changed her plans to dance—not ever. This would be a first.

"I can dance in the ski lodge," Aimee answered. "Can't I?"

They gave each other a big hug and headed toward school.

As they entered the school building, Madison and Aimee felt as if they had slammed into a force field. They had been happily bouncing down the street, but once inside FHJH the vibe was grouchy. The plague that everyone had caught was the winter blahs. Fortunately, most of the teachers understood that no one wanted to be in real classes, so they had the students play classroom games like bingo or charades. Others showed movies over two or three class periods. Gradually, as the morning progressed, people's moods lifted.

Just before the lunch break, Madison spoke to Aimee outside the girls' bathroom on the third floor. As they stood there, Hart sauntered by. Madison gushed about the spontaneous ski trip. Hart was impressed.

"Wow, I didn't know you skied!" Hart said. "My

family went up to Big Mountain once. It's really nice there. You're lucky."

"Did you hear that?" Aimee squealed. "We're lucky!"

"Lucky us! Lucky us!" Madison chanted.

Hart squinted and glanced around the hallway to see who was looking their way. He obviously didn't want to be seen next to a pair of screaming girls.

"Um . . . could you guys . . . um . . . keep it down?" Hart said.

"What's *your* prob?" Aimee shouted. "I'm not keeping anything down! I'm going skiing, I'm going skiing! Wahoo! Maybe there'll be some cute boys on the slopes."

Now Hart looked utterly embarrassed.

Madison gulped. Had he heard Aimee's "cute boys on the slopes" comment?

"Hart," Madison blurted out, not really knowing what to say next.

"Yeah?" Hart said, looking right back at her.

"Hart, you'd better . . . um . . ." Madison was stuck.

"I'd better *go*?" Hart said, raising his eyebrows. "I know. I heard what Aimee said."

Madison's chest heaved. Although she had made up her mind the night before to go on a Hart boycott, this wasn't how she had wanted to do it.

But she didn't have a chance to make things right, because Egg showed up. And then Drew Maxwell, Egg's friend, appeared, too. Fiona and

Chet soon followed. Now it wasn't just a few friends standing there—it was a whole cluster.

The moment between Madison and Hart was gone, and Madison didn't get to finish what she had meant to say. She looked over at Hart, who had moved away from her.

"So, you're going skiing," Drew said to Madison.

Madison shrugged. "Yup. Me and Aimee."

"Maddie, I am totally jealous of you both," Fiona said. "I wish I didn't have to go to California. Skiing sounds so much cooler than surfing."

"It does?" Madison asked.

"Well, duh," Egg said. "Of course it's cooler. There's snow involved."

Drew snorted. He laughed at almost everything Egg said.

"I know! Maddie, Fiona, and I will e-mail each other the whole time we're on the trip," Aimee said. She'd already figured everything out: how they'd keep in touch; what she was going to wear; what they were going to do; and whom they were going to see.

"You mean e-mail from my laptop?" Madison asked.

"Well, you are bringing it, right?" Aimee asked.

"You have to take lots of pictures, too!" Fiona said. "Doesn't your dad have a digital camera, Maddie?"

Madison nodded. She looked over at Hart again. He was staring back at her. There was no doubt about it. Maybe he wanted to say something more, like: "Don't go!" or "I'll miss you."

But neither Madison nor Hart spoke a single word more to each other.

Madison took another deep breath.

The bell sounded in the hall, and everyone scrambled to head for their classes. Fiona pulled Madison and Aimee over to the side before they could walk away.

"Look what I brought!" Fiona said to her friends. She pulled out a ministack of yellow letters. "I made copies of Aim's chain letter on my dad's scanner," she said. "And he had some extra yellow paper in his home office—just like the original letter."

"No way!" Aimee said, trying to keep her voice low and shield the pages from any roaming eyes in the hallway.

Madison was pleased. At least sending copies of Aimee's chain letter meant they were following the scary "pass this along to five more people" rule. That meant they would have good luck. Fiona had even added a date that had *already passed* to the top of the letter, so that Poison Ivy would get her copy and think she'd missed the chain-letter deadline. It was a perfect plan! Poison Ivy would definitely freak out if she suspected terrible luck coming her way.

A teacher came up to the three BFFs and crossed her arms sternly. "Excuse me, girls," she said. "The bell rang. Get back to your classrooms."

Madison waved to Aimee and Fiona and disappeared down the hall. "E me later!" she said to her friends.

"Forget E. I'll *see* you later!" Aimee giggled.

At home later that night, Madison pulled on two pairs of striped socks to keep her feet warm. Temperatures had dropped during the evening. The weather report had said there was going to be snow.

Before packing her ski-trip suitcase, Madison went online to check her e-mailbox. What a surprise! There were three e-mails. Two were from a store that sold toys at half price after the holidays. Madison hit DELETE. Junk e-mail clogged the e-mailbox, and Madison needed to make room for real mail. There was, however, one real note from her faraway keypal, Bigwheels.

From: Bigwheels
To: MadFinn
Subject: I Still Have a Cold
Date: Wed 24 Feb 6:43 PM
___
It's official. I've been out of
school for a week. I have never had
a sore throat for this long. And I
never thought I would say this, but
I am actually getting sick of TV.
They show the same movies over and
over again.

But that's not the worst of it. My brother and sister r sick 2 so who do you think gets all the TLC? If you answer ME you're wrong. Ur so lucky 2 B an only child.

Hey r u still planning to redo your computer filing system over the school vacation? I wish we had school vacations @ the same time. Then I could come visit you and we could hang out together and talk and stuff. I would be soooo GTSY! And i could meet Hart!!! BTW: how is he?

OMG I just sneezed all over my keyboard. That is so gross. OK. G2G!

Yours till the temperature rises,

Bigwheels aka Sneezy

Madison laughed to herself and hit REPLY.

From: MadFinn
To: Bigwheels
Subject: Re: I Still Have a Cold
Date: Wed 24 Feb 8:29 PM

Bless you! You sneezed, right? LOL I am so not redoing my filing this vacation and do you know why? I AM

GOING SKIING AT A FOUR-STAR
RESORT!!!

My dad surprised me yesterday
with the news. He's taking me &
my BFF Aimee to this place called
Big Mountain it's way up in NY
somewhere, up near Canada almost.
I heard movie stars even go there
sometimes. I dunno. Maybe I'll
meet someone famous and fall madly
in love and OOTB you'll see me on
the cover of Star Beat! YEAH,
RIGHT!!!

Oh yeah, about Hart. Well . . .
I still like him. I think. He's
acting so weird lately. I just
don't think our relationship is
going anywhere. For starters, we
haven't exactly established it as a
relationship. I know he likes me. I
think. It's a little confusing.
Aimee says I should check out other
boys and get a new crush. What do u
think I should do? Ur always good
w/that stuff.

I wish u had the same vacation as
me. WE could have gone skiing
together! U could see me fall

on my face in a big snowdrift
LOL b/c I am not a very good skier.
I'm not a very good dresser for
the ski slopes either which could
be a problem considering how fancy
shmancy this place is supposed to
be. Right now I am about to start
packing and my room is a disaster
and . . . I better go! TTYL.

Yours till the ski boots,

Maddie

p.s.: -=#:-)/

that's the wizard and his wand to
wave all your sickness away--isn't
that fun? my friend sent it 2 me

After closing her e-mailbox, Madison clicked on a search engine. If she was going to have any luck at all packing for the last-minute trip, she needed some ideas. Out of curiosity, she plugged in the words *ski wardrobe* and got 61,800 hits. She was bound to get some stylin' ideas from one of those sites. Madison clicked on the first three.

SKI WARDROBE... **SKI** ACCESSORIES... **SKI** FASHION FIXES... comes with stormflap,

2 lower zipped warm lined pockets, lightly insulated for your **ski wardrobe**...

SKIYOUMAMA **SKI**WEAR WHERE YOU BE COOL ON THE SLOPES
Ski Wardrobe: Fleece hats, snowboards, headbands, scarves, fleece socks, mittens, and items that make perfect gifts

GREAT LEAP **SKI** RESORT WEAR FOR YOUR **SKI WARDROBE**
Average snow cover of 143 cm during the **ski** season. More **Ski** Runs. Length, vertical drop, difficulty, **ski** lift.

"This is hopeless," Madison said as she moved her cursor across the screen. "I don't know where to look for fashion ideas. I don't have a fleece snowboard hat. I don't even know what that is."

She read the Skiyoumama site's page, called Fashion Tips. It said, "The color graphite is all the rage on the slopes, with moss, slate, pale gold, ice blue, and lilac also showing up."

"Graphite? Moss?" Madison wondered aloud, flashing a look at her own closet. She was lucky to have one jacket hanging there that she could use for skiing. And it was plain old dark blue.

It was probably time to call Aimee and ask for

packing advice. Madison was certain that her appearance on the slopes at Big Mountain would not be a major fashion event, but she didn't want to be a *complete* geek, either. There must be something in her closet that would look good.

Aimee was happy to help.

"Okay, first . . ." Aimee instructed on the telephone. "First, you need to have your basics, Maddie. Faded jeans . . ."

Madison wandered over to her closet and picked up a pair from the laundry pile. "Um . . ." she said. She tossed them onto her bed. "Got 'em."

"Now," Aimee said, "what about sweaters? And dresses? And that little corduroy skirt you have? You could wear that with cable-knit tights and those cool boots you got last Christmas."

"Huh?" Madison looked around. "I don't know where the skirt is. I don't even know if it fits me anymore, Aim."

"That's okay. We'll try another look," Aimee said, sounding a lot like a makeover expert on a reality TV show. She listed more items for Madison to pack. Unfortunately, most of the clothes on Aimee's list were nowhere to be found in Madison's room. Madison felt as though her closet were nothing more than a vast fashion wasteland. She could almost see the tumbleweeds.

"Rowwooooooooof!" Phin barked at Madison and the phone.

"Maddie? Is that you?" Aimee yelled into the phone.

"Phin!" Madison cried as the dog barked again and buried his wet nose in one of her sneakers. It was bad enough that she didn't have the clothes Aimee was suggesting, but to have doggy drool all over the outfits that she *did* have? That was too much.

"Aim, I have to go," Madison gasped into the receiver. "Phin's being a pest. Give me ten minutes, and I'll call you back, 'kay?"

She hung up the phone and burrowed in to a pile of sweaters that had tumbled down from a shelf. Phin came over and pounced on her back. As he squiggled around, Phin caught his paws on a blue cardigan sweater with wooden buttons. It looked like something Madison might have worn in second grade. Now, it was a definite *no*.

Then, from the pile, Madison saw some clothes that would work. She yanked out a zip-up red hoodie that Stephanie had bought for her at the mall. She also found an old pair of red snow pants that had been buried way in the back of her closet.

Two items down, twenty to go.

Her suitcase was filling up slowly—but at least it was filling up.

Chapter 3

"Maddie, honey," Mom whispered in a groggy voice. "Honey bear, it's almost dawn."

Phin was still snoring. Lucky dog. He didn't have to get up until everything was already packed into the car.

Madison crawled out of bed and got into the shower. She'd managed to pack her suitcase the night before but hadn't fallen asleep until after eleven-thirty, and now . . .

All she could do was yawn.

Dad would be there in an hour.

Madison brushed her teeth, staring back at her own glassy-eyed reflection in the mirror. Bathroom light was the most unflattering light on the planet—

especially at five in the morning. Madison wanted to crawl back into bed.

She pulled on a pair of cargo pants, a pale yellow T-shirt, and a green zip-up fleece top that Dad had bought her in downtown Far Hills. It was warm. She was sleepy. That made an ideal combination. Her hair was misbehaving, so Madison yanked it back into a pink elastic and washed her face. She still couldn't get the taste of sleep out of her mouth, so she grabbed the mouthwash from Mom's bathroom. Had she been up this early in the morning—ever?

Phin followed Madison downstairs. She was moving like Frankenstein's monster, all stiff-legged, and Phin almost tripped over her feet.

Ding-dong. Ding-dong.

"I'll get it!" Madison called out, as if Mom had had any intention of getting the door. Mom had sprawled back across her own bed with the words: "Wake me when your dad gets here."

Madison went to the door and opened it. On the porch landing stood Aimee, her purple suitcase on wheels waiting next to her.

"Ready, spaghetti?" Aimee said. She was awfully perky for that early in the morning, Madison thought. And her hair looked perfect, nothing like Madison's bed head.

"Nhhhunnnh," Madison grunted. "Morning."

"You look so good! I'm so excited. Aren't you so excited? I can't believe you asked me to go with you.

You are the *best*!" She leaned into Madison and gave her a big hug.

"No problem," Madison said.

Aimee stepped inside the front door. "Can you wait a sec? I just have to pee," she said with a smile, and she dashed for the downstairs bathroom.

Madison sat in a chair in the hall and cradled her head in her hands. Phin jumped up onto her lap, panting, his little tongue hanging out. She closed her eyes. It would be fine once they were on the road with Dad and Stephanie, but at the moment, Madison could still feel the magnetic pull of her bed . . . *sleeeeeeep*! She couldn't deal with a chipper best friend *and* dog.

"I love those pants!" Aimee said when she bounded back out of the bathroom. "You've never worn those before. Have you ever worn those before?"

Aimee wore a purple heather turtleneck sweater, flared cutoffs, and black leather boots. Well, they weren't *real* leather. The health-conscious Gillespie family only bought things made of fake leather. It looked a lot like the real thing, though.

Madison's mom shuffled down the stairs into the hallway. "Hey, girls," she mumbled. "How are you, Aimee? Have you eaten breakfast yet? Why don't I fix you both some juice and cereal?"

Aimee grinned. "Sure!" she said. "Some OJ would be cool."

Madison's stomach grumbled, but she couldn't even think about food. The sun was barely up.

They sat together at the kitchen table. Mom turned on the radio and a soft disco beat filled the room.

"This is 'Ask Me How I Feel'! I love this song," Aimee said. "Can you turn it up?"

Soon the room was filled with soft yellow light. As Mom turned up the radio, Madison yawned and stretched. Sleep was finally fading.

"Come on, Maddie!" Aimee shouted, jumping up to dance.

Phinnie chased Aimee's feet as she moved from side to side; his little tail wagged behind him.

Madison rubbed her eyes and laughed. "Aim, it's six o'clock in the morning. I'm beat. How can you dance?"

"Any time is a good time to dance," Aimee said, shaking her hips. She pulled Madison up to dance. "Besides, isn't this your favorite song?" she asked.

Madison started to giggle as she attempted to shake her hips, too. But her rhythm was a little off this morning. Even Phin was dancing better than she was.

Mom smiled. "I wish I had my camera. You girls crack me up. You're so beautiful. . . ."

"Beautiful? Oh, Mom," Madison sighed. "Don't get all mushy on me now."

"I still can't believe we're really, truly going to

Big Mountain," Aimee said. "I read in *Star Beat* that Foster Lane spends his weekends there in the winter."

"Foster Lane? Is that a real name? Who's he?" Mom asked.

Aimee feigned disbelief. Her jaw dropped open. "Mrs. Finn!" she exclaimed. "Foster is a major hottie. He's on that TV show *Lost in Tucson*."

"Whoa," Mom said, chuckling. "I thought I was pretty hip, but I've never heard of him or his show. And I work in the movie business!"

Madison laughed. "Wait! I'm starting to get that weird butterfly feeling," she said. "Right here." Madison pointed to her stomach.

"I know. Me, too," Aimee said. "This trip is the deal."

Ding-dong.

"And there's your dad!" Aimee squealed.

Mom zipped up the canvas bag with Phin's dog food and chew toys in it. She set aside his beanbag for sleeping, although there probably wasn't enough room in Dad's car for it. Dad had rented a Jeep for driving up to the mountains. Some luggage could go on top of the car, some would be stacked in the back, but it would be a tight squeeze with the five of them: Dad, Stephanie, Madison, Aimee, and Phineas T. Finn.

"You girls ready?" Dad called out from the hallway. He'd let himself in at the front door, which wasn't really all that weird, considering the fact that this had once been his house, too. Madison still felt strange when he rang the doorbell.

"Dad!" Madison yelled as she ran for the door. She gave him a big hug. So did Aimee.

"I should be around for most of the week," Mom said. "If you need anything."

"Thank you, Francine," Dad said.

Madison grabbed her two smaller bags. Aimee rolled her suitcase back out onto the porch. Mom kissed Maddie, Aimee, and Phin good-bye.

"I packed his little doggy sweater," Mom said. "The one that Gramma Helen knit for him."

"Awwwww, that is so-o-o-o-o sweet!" Aimee said.

Even though Madison was feeling much more alert, Aimee's high-pitched squeals were still a little over the top.

Everyone said a second round of good-byes and then the travelers headed for the car. Stephanie was inside, half covered by a wool blanket.

"Good morning," Madison said as she squeezed into the back. It was a snug fit. Phin wasn't sure where he was supposed to go. Finally, he curled up in a ball on Madison's lap. Aimee got in on the other side.

Madison stared out the window as they pulled away. By now, the sky was white with morning light. Trucks headed for delivery stops. City buses chugged along on their early-morning routes. There were only a few other cars along the road.

They passed the Far Hills Animal Clinic, where Madison liked to volunteer. They even drove past a tomblike Far Hills Junior High.

"It's official. We're really on winter break," Madison said with a sigh. "I never thought it would come, but now it's here. And we're leaving town!"

"Um . . . can we listen to the radio?" Aimee asked.

"Sure," Stephanie said. She clicked on a station. "Ask Me How I Feel" was playing.

"No way!" Aimee cried.

"The same song!" Madison screamed.

Dad jumped. The car lurched. Phin scrambled into the front seat.

"Phin! Madison!" Dad groaned. He used her full first name only when he was annoyed at something.

"Oh, sorry, Dad," Madison said. "It's just that this song was playing on the radio at Mom's, too, just a few minutes ago, and if you randomly hear the same song like that, it means that it's your lucky song. Doesn't it, Aim?"

"You're the one who believes in all that superstitious stuff," Aimee said.

"Well," Dad said, "I don't care if it is your lucky song. That's no reason to scream in the car. I thought something was wrong."

Aimee made a "whoopsie" face. Madison squirmed in her seat.

They drove on. Once they hit the highway, everyone (except Dad, of course) started to doze off.

Madison awoke half an hour later with a cramp in her leg. Stephanie was looking out the window, or sleeping—Madison couldn't tell. Phin slept on Stephanie's lap. Dad was listening to talk radio, not the cool music station they'd been listening to before. Aimee was still out cold, her mouth hanging open the way it usually did when she slept. She always slept funny. Once, at a sleepover, Madison, Fiona, and their other friend Lindsay watched as Aimee rolled over, mouth open, asleep, onto her giant teddy bear. The next day, Aimee woke up with fur on her tongue.

"Daddy?" Madison asked softly from the back seat. "I'm going to use my laptop. Is that okay?"

"Of course," he said. "That's why I got you the laptop. So you could take it anywhere you wanted."

"I mean, is it okay if we don't talk?" Madison asked. "I don't want you to think I'm being rude or that I don't want to talk or . . . well, you know what I mean."

Dad looked briefly over his shoulder at her and then turned back to the road. He could see Madison through his rearview mirror.

"Maddie, this is your vacation," he said. "Do whatever you want."

Madison logged on and opened a new file.

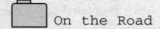 On the Road

Rude Awakening: I thought taking a trip with Dad and Stephanie would drive me crazy. But this vacation feels like it's driving in a very different direction.

Big news: in addition to keeping her mouth wide open like a trout, Aimee snores! I never knew that, even after all the times I slept over at her house and she slept over at mine. Or maybe she snores because she is sitting up. I wish I had my video so I had proof. She will totally deny that she does this.

I forgot that once you drive out of Far Hills, there are so many trees and mountains, and everything here is dusted with snow. Dad says that when we get up to the Adirondack mountains, we'll be climbing in altitude. It gets colder, so there's even more snow on the ground. He's good with all that science data. I know he watches the Weather Channel a lot.

Oh, wow! As I'm writing this, we just passed this HUGE farm with cows everywhere. And I can see there's a flurry of snow in the air now. Stephanie's waking up in the front seat. She rolled down her window for a little fresh air and WHAMMO! A gust of snowy air blew right into her face. Between the snow and the snores, this is pretty

funny stuff. But I'm trying desperately not
to laugh back here.

I have absolutely less than no idea
where we are, except that we just passed a
sign that said "ALBANY, 40 Miles" and I
know that's the state capital. So we must
be more than halfway there. Dad said it
takes five hours.

Madison glanced over at Aimee, who was still snoring. Stephanie heard the snoring, too, and smiled at Madison from the front seat.

"Do you want to hold Phin?" she asked.

Madison nodded and carefully took the pug onto her lap.

"I think we'll stop up ahead," Dad said. "There's a rest stop. We can grab some coffee or soda and take a bathroom break."

Phin pressed his pug nose up against the back window, and it steamed up. The air was definitely getting colder. A light snow had begun to fall.

As they pulled off the road into a rest stop, Aimee finally woke up. "Where are we?" she asked, rubbing her eyes. "Look! It's snowing!"

Outside, flurries were starting to fall faster now. It was as though they'd driven onto a movie set or into a giant Christmas card.

Everyone grabbed a drink and a snack at the rest stop, and then they headed out on to the road again. Dad was struggling a little bit with the map.

He was looking for a shortcut to the resort. His client had given him directions for the back-road route, but Dad couldn't seem to find one of the country roads he was looking for.

"Jeff, dear, take the main highway," Stephanie advised sweetly.

Madison already knew what was going to happen—and it wasn't pretty. Dad always refused to do things the easy way.

About a half hour after leaving the rest stop, Madison leaned over to Aimee and whispered, "We're lost. I can feel it."

"I heard that!" Dad snapped from the front. "We are not lost. I'm just taking the scenic route. I think the snow's letting up."

Stephanie chuckled. "Oh, Jeff, the snow is the least of our worries."

Kerthunk.

The car moved shakily from side to side.

"What was that?" Aimee cried from the back.

"Yes, Jeff, what *was* that?" Stephanie asked, clutching her car door. "Was that the tire?"

"Rowwrooooo-rorrrroroooooo!" Phin barked.

Dad sat forward in his seat and gently applied the brake. "I have no idea what the—"

Kerplonk.

"Now, that didn't sound like a flat tire. Did it?" Dad asked.

"It sounded bad," Aimee responded.

"You can fix it. Right, Dad?" Madison asked.

All at once, the car lurched forward and then slowed down to a crawl. Dad guided it over to the side of the road. The five of them (including Phinnie) sat there quietly.

Dad pounded his fist on of the dashboard. "This is just my luck!" he cried.

Stephanie put her hand on his arm. "Don't worry, Jeff."

Madison liked the way her stepmother acted in stressful situations. Stephanie's cooler-than-cool demeanor calmed Dad down. Madison remembered how different it had been between Mom and Dad. On family trips, they would make each other *more* stressed.

"So . . . are we going to get out of the car?" Aimee asked Madison. She looked over at her friend.

"I don't know," Madison said with a shrug.

"Let's call triple A first," Stephanie said. The American Automobile Association helped cars in emergencies like this. One call would summon a tow truck and mechanic to come and help fix the car.

"Oh, no." Dad stared straight ahead at the steering wheel. "You won't believe this, Stephanie. I left my card in my other wallet."

"You forgot your card? When we were taking a major road trip?" Stephanie said. "Jeff, how could you do that?"

Madison and Aimee didn't say a word more.

Dad hung his head. "We were so rushed, I just—"

"Here, use *my* card," Stephanie said, pulling it out of her purse with a smile.

Dad leaned over and brushed Stephanie's cheek with his hand. "Thank you," he said.

When they got out of the Jeep, everyone saw the problem right away: not just one but *two* very flat tires.

Dad and Stephanie walked down the road a short distance to get better reception on the cell phone. Madison and Aimee waited near the car. Phin sniffed around the flat tires.

"Hey, Aim, do you see that?" Madison asked Aimee, pointing into the sky.

Aimee was too busy primping to notice. Her hair and outfit had gotten mussed when she fell asleep in the backseat.

Madison craned her neck to look up into the sky. Right above the Jeep, a group of crows circled around. They cawed loudly. She wondered if it were a bad omen.

Were flat tires and crows signs of bad luck that couldn't be shaken?

Was the trip to Big Mountain headed for big problems?

Chapter 4

"I'm cold," Aimee complained after they'd stood in the road for twenty minutes.

"So, why don't you put on another sweater," Madison suggested.

Aimee rubbed her eyes. "I'm tired, too," she moaned. She sat down on the Jeep's bumper. "How long do you think we'll have to wait?" she asked.

Madison shrugged. It already felt as if they'd been waiting forever. She scanned the sky again for the crows, but they seemed to have flown away. She hoped that that was a good sign.

Dad and Stephanie sat on a large boulder a short distance from the car, waiting impatiently for the tow truck to appear.

Madison grabbed Phin's leash tightly as the dog paraded around the Jeep, sniffing the area. He shivered a little, so Madison pulled him up into her arms, rubbing his little paws. They were half frozen from contact with the cold ground.

"We should have gotten Phinnie little fleece ski boots," Madison joked loudly. "Right, Dad?"

Dad wasn't laughing. He had his nose buried in the car manual that he'd found inside the glove compartment.

Stephanie, however, smiled. She stood up and walked over to the BFFs. "How are you gals holding up?" Stephanie asked. She put her arm around Madison's shoulders and squeezed.

"Aimee's cold," Madison answered. "We're so scrunched in the backseat, too. Usually, road trips are cool, but for some reason . . ."

"Oh, I guess we should have rented a larger minivan," Stephanie said. "Next time we'll know better."

Madison wondered how Stephanie could be thinking about a next time when this time had scarcely begun.

"Aimee, have you skied much?" Stephanie asked.

"A little bit," Aimee said. "My brothers are all way better than me. I tried snowboarding a few times, though. I was okay at that."

"Wow, snowboarding! That's very impressive," Stephanie said. "I'd like to try that. I've gone surfing a few times in Hawaii but never snowboarded."

"You've been to Hawaii?" Aimee cried. "That's, like, my dream vacation."

Madison thought about surfing and how Fiona was probably halfway to California by then, not stuck on the side of some mountain in the middle of nowhere, waiting for a massive snowstorm to swallow her up.

A loud boom came from down the road behind them. A silver tow truck pulled into view, engines rumbling, red and yellow lights flashing.

The driver poked his elbow and then his head out of the window.

"Ahoy, there!" he said, as if he were standing on the stern of a ship. His face was grizzled and he wore a brown baseball cap that read MOE'S TRUCK STOP. "Got yerself a flat, do you?"

"We have *two*," Dad moaned. "Can you beat that?"

The driver and Dad surveyed the damage and made arrangements to head to a nearby service station. The closest one was twelve miles back in the opposite direction. Dad and Phin drove to the station in the cab of the tow truck. Stephanie, Madison, and Aimee got a special ride in another car sent by the garage.

Once they got there, it took a long time for the Jeep to be repaired. Stephanie took Phin for a walk. Aimee and Madison hung out inside the service station and got cups of hot cocoa from a vending machine.

"It's just not the same as Mom's, is it?" Madison joked as the machine spit gobs of brown stuff into the cups and squirted a dollop of fake whipped cream on top of each one. The cream melted before they could even take sips, but they drank up anyway.

A pair of drab green plastic chairs stood in the corner of the room. Madison pulled her laptop out of her bag and took a seat. Aimee sat down, too.

"The other day I found this cool Web site," Madison explained. "It's called Love Connection. You punch in the name of the person you really like, and it tells you whether you have a perfect love match or not."

"Those games don't mean anything," Aimee said with a toss of her head. "You don't believe them, do you?"

"What are you talking about?" Madison said. "Of course I do."

"Maddie, that's like writing your names and counting the vowels to see if you're destined to be together," Aimee said.

"Yeah, what's wrong with that? I do that all the time," Madison said. "I can't believe you don't do that. Everyone does that."

"Whatever," Aimee said. "Go ahead and log on. I'll play."

Madison booted up the computer and typed the Web site address in to her browser. A screen flashed the sentence WHAT'S YOUR LOVE CONNECTION?

Background music played. Little pink hearts danced around the border of the page. The screen prompted Madison to enter the name of her crush and her own name.

Madison stared at the screen.

"Well, what are you waiting for?" Aimee asked. "Put in 'Hart Jones.'"

"But you said I'm supposed to get a new crush," Madison said.

"So? See if you and Hart are destined to be together anyway," Aimee insisted. "It's only a game."

"I thought you said you didn't believe in this stuff," Madison said.

"Yeah, well . . . maybe I believe in it a little," Aimee admitted with a smile. "Plug in Hart's name. Go ahead."

Madison entered the names. The screen flashed, and then the results popped up.

Hart Jones and Madison Finn:
26% chance of romance

Madison's face drooped when she saw that.

"That's terrible," Madison said.

"Oh, Maddie, it doesn't mean anything," Aimee said. "It's just a number."

"A low number," Madison said with a sigh. In that moment, she felt as though all the time she had spent liking Hart had been wasted; as though she should have been crushing on someone who had a better percentage.

Aimee leaned over and typed in another name next to Madison's. Before Madison could erase it, the Web site flashed the new message.

Walter Diaz and Madison Finn:
85% chance of romance

Madison gasped. "Aimee! I could kill you! How could you type in Egg's name! That is so gross! I'm glad Fiona isn't here. She'd kill me!"

Madison quickly typed *Aimee Gillespie* over her own name. She typed *Benjamin Buckley* in to the *boy* slot. Aimee tried to hit the DELETE key but she wasn't fast enough.

Benjamin Buckley and Aimee Gillespie:
74% chance of romance

Aimee raised her eyebrows. "Not bad," she said. "Now, if only Ben knew what romance was," she giggled.

"It's way better than 26 percent," Madison groaned, recalling the low number she'd received for Hart. Madison typed in a new pair of names.

Hart Jones and Ivy Daly:
81% chance of romance

Madison felt as though she'd been choked. She couldn't breathe. How could Ivy have such a good number?

Dad walked over, rubbing his hands together. He was finally grinning, after a morning of grouchiness.

"Grab your gear, girls," Dad said. "Car's fixed."

Madison closed her laptop, and she and Aimee headed back to the car.

Stephanie was already inside. Phin had stretched out across her lap, gnawing on a rawhide chew toy.

An hour and a half later, after a few rounds of I Spy and tic-tac-toe, they played a few more games of Love Connection, and Madison discovered that her ideal love connection was a dweeby guy named Philip Ayres, who sat a row away from her in math class. She decided that the Web site had to be rigged. There was no way that that boy could be her true love. She eventually got the bright idea of typing in Hart's name and her name with *middle* names included, which vastly improved their percentages. With middle names included, Hart Jefferson Jones and Madison Francesca Finn had an 81 percent chance of romance—the same percentage Ivy had gotten.

"Here we are!" Stephanie called out as they drove past the sign that welcomed them to ELK LAKE: HOME OF BIG MOUNTAIN SKI AREA.

"I know the entrance is coming up. It's a private resort, so there's no big sign," Dad said. "Keep your eyes open, girls, for Treetops."

Madison, Aimee, and Stephanie all looked from side to side for their destination. After ten minutes, they still had not found it. Dad decided that they had probably missed it, so he turned the car around.

That was when Madison spotted the small green sign, shaped like an evergreen tree.

TREETOPS. PRIVATE CLUB. MEMBERS ONLY.

Dad made a quick right turn and skidded on the gravel. The Jeep bounded down a bumpy road toward the main lodge. On either side of the road was melted snow, probably left over from a previous snowstorm. They drove along until Dad reached a fork in the road.

"Which way?" Dad asked.

Stephanie laughed as Dad veered off to the left.

"Mr. Finn!" Aimee said, laughing in the backseat.

Madison looked out the car window. There were trees as far as the eye could see. Where was the lodge? Where were all the other guests? Why hadn't they seen another car in more than ten minutes?

Outside, atop a pile of snow, Madison spotted something moving. It was black. A cat? Her heart filled with dread. The last thing they needed was another bad omen—and a black cat was just about the worst one she could imagine.

Thankfully, it was just a black squirrel. It dashed away into the forest.

"Holy cow!" Dad cried as they pulled into a clearing. "Where did this place come from?"

The Treetops Lodge came into view. It looked like a castle. A great, wide porch encircled the main building. Hanging over the main entryway was a pair of enormous snowshoes. Lights shaped like stars hung from the rafters.

Contrary to the impression the quiet entry road had given, this place wasn't deserted at all. Off to the side, a couple of men stood with shovels. A couple wearing mirrored sunglasses kissed each other before getting into their car. A group of women in colorful ski parkas and knitted caps waved to an oncoming group of men in just as colorful parkas and caps.

"Welcome to Treetops, sir, may we help you?" a man said to Dad as they pulled up in front.

Since it was valet parking only, Madison, Aimee, Stephanie, Dad, and Phin got out of the car and emptied the trunk. A porter loaded the bags onto a rolling cart and guided it inside.

"This is first class," Dad whispered to Stephanie. "I can't believe we're here."

Stephanie beamed. She fit right into the crowd at the lodge in her shiny black parka with its white fake-fur trim. She looked up at Dad. "I feel like part of a real family. Thank you," she said.

Madison and Aimee squeezed each other's hands but didn't say much. There was too much to look at. The main lodge was surrounded by small roads and paths, outer buildings that looked like minilodges, and a great atrium that looked like an indoor conservatory or greenhouse.

The large wooden sign in front of the main lodge read: TREETOPS GUIDE. Underneath were sheets of yellow paper that listed the events at the lodge. Madison and Aimee read the postings.

Cross-Country Skiing
Nordic ski trails in the area may be explored alone or with a professional guide for half the day or for a full day. Daily shuttle service is available each hour to Big Mountain, where you may spend the day on numerous cross-country trails.

Downhill Skiing and Snowboarding
Ski and ride a spectacular vertical drop in the east at Big Mountain.

Dogsled Rides
Enjoy a dogsled ride on the ice of Elk Lake surrounded by the Adirondack mountains. Leaves at 11 A.M. daily.

Ice Fishing
Guided ice fishing trips for beginners and advanced leaves at 7 A.M. Breakfast served on the way.

Sleigh Ride Dinners
Take a horse-drawn sleigh ride accompanied with champagne dinner. Make reservations at the front desk.

"Did you read that?" Aimee exclaimed. "Dog-sleds? Ice fishing? I thought that only happened in Alaska or the North Pole! How cool would a sleigh-ride dinner be? Did your dad say if we'd be doing that?"

"Aim, get real. A sleigh ride is for couples," Madison said, frowning. "Not for kids like you and me."

"Fine. But do you think Phin would like the dogsled ride?" Aimee asked.

They giggled.

Off to the side were smaller signposts pointing out the way to all of the other buildings and sights on the Treetops property. Madison could see the names: Iroquois, Kiwasa, and Mohawk. Somewhere, nestled in these woods, was their own private lodge. Madison couldn't wait to see it.

Dad and Stephanie finally exited the main lodge with the keys to their rooms. Their reservation was for Eagle's Nest, a much smaller lodge right down by the shores of one of the lakes on the property. It was only a short walk away. Dad said that when it snowed, the lodge sent over skimobiles for trans-portation.

By then, the air had gotten chillier. Night was on its way. Madison and Aimee walked arm in arm toward Eagle's Nest, sticking close together to stay warm.

The interior of the lodge was even more beauti-ful than Madison could have imagined. The ceiling was at least fifteen feet high, with skylights and windows all around, looking onto a quiet, dark lake lit by the white moon. A giant stone fireplace rose up from the center of the room. Off to the side was the main bedroom, where a huge bed stood with legs that looked like tree roots growing right out of the floor. A smaller room contained twin beds for Madison and Aimee and even a little doggy bed.

Dad had not been kidding when he'd said the lodge catered to people with pets, Madison thought. Phin was going to love this place.

Madison threw herself across a plush sofa in front of the fireplace. The smell and sound of the wood burning in the fireplace gave her a warm feeling all over. Despite its rocky beginning, the day was ending well.

"I have to call home," Aimee said, taking a seat next to Madison. "My mom will not believe it when I tell her about this place. It's amazing."

"I'm sure Stephanie will let you use her cell phone," Madison said.

"Sure thing. Here you go," Stephanie said, handing the phone to Aimee.

While Aimee talked to her parents, Madison stretched out on the couch. She was feeling luckier than lucky to be in such a great place. But when Aimee got off the phone she looked a little sad.

Madison grabbed her friend by the arm. "Are you okay?" she asked.

Aimee smiled. "I'm fine," she said. "Just missing home for some weird reason. Not a lot, but a little. Is that dumb?"

"No," Madison said. She gave her friend a big hug.

Then the two dragged their suitcases into the room, unpacked, washed up, and crawled under the covers.

"I know we're tired. But do you want to see if Fiona's online?" Madison asked.

"What a great idea!" Aimee said.

Madison booted up her laptop. Fiona *was* online.

<MadFinn>: Fiona! We MISS u! (me
   and Aim)
<Wetwinz>: I can't believe u guys
   r online I just was on the
   computer for only ten minutes to
   check my e-mail OMG how is the
   trip????
<MadFinn>: Aim says to tell u it's
   ok except she misses BB
<Wetwinz>: Ben Buckley? Wait she did
   NOT say that
<MadFinn>: LOL she just punched me
   in the shoulder. So how was the
   hockey game?
<Wetwinz>: we lost but only by one
   goal. Chet is bummed
<MadFinn>: how's hart? :>)
<Wetwinz>: he got a goal in the

game and so did Egg. Hart asked
about u BTW
<MadFinn>: he did?
<Wetwinz>: I think u should send
him a postcard, maddie, so he
doesn't think ur mad at him. He
told egg that he thinks ur acting
weird l8ly
<MadFinn>: WAIT Fiona this is Aimee
typin now and Hart is just bogus
I mean we already decided maddie
is getting a new crush so we have
2 4get about Hart and the reason
she's acting weird is b/c HE IS
WEIRDER
<Wetwinz>: WAM! I think he's sweet
<MadFinn>: oh u think everyone is
sweet
<Wetwinz>: aim ur so negative. Tell
me what is the ski place like I'm
sooooo curious
<MadFinn>: hey Fiona it's maddie
typing again--and please please
FORGET what Aimee said just now,
like DON'T tell Hart or Egg
<Wetwinz>: I promise I won't tell
404
<MadFinn>: thanks
<Wetwinz>: it must be soooooo cold
there
<MadFinn>: <brrrrr>

```
<Wetwinz>: I wish I could c it
<MadFinn>: I have my dad's digital
    camera I'll E u a picture
<Wetwinz>: thanx
<MadFinn>: BTW Aim sez to say we
    MISS U
<Wetwinz>: me 2
<MadFinn>: E us when u get to
    CA!!!!
<Wetwinz>: yeah E me when you find
    ur new crush
```

They said their good-byes, and Madison logged off. She gave Aimee another poke in the arm.

"I can't believe you said that stuff about Hart!" Madison said.

"Well, it's true, isn't it?" Aimee replied.

Madison leaned back against the down comforter. She wasn't sure what was true about her feelings anymore.

But she was hoping a little snow and skiing might help her figure it out.

Chapter 5

The Lodge

SNOOOOOOW! Woke up this morning and looked outside. During the night everything got covered in snow and it reminded me of when I was a little kid and Mom used to tell me that Frosty came during the night when I slept. There were icicles like spiderwebs in all the trees.

Aimee is asleep right now in the next bed. Phin is curled up by her head. They're both snoring a little. I'm staying under the blankets as long as I possibly can and then we get to go SKIING! Yeah! Could this be more perfect? And I was afraid of a little bad omen.

"Oh, my goodness!" Stephanie screamed from the other room. "Oh, no!"

Madison jumped, clutching her computer. Phin and Aimee woke up, startled.

"Jeff, come and look! It snowed!" Stephanie said.

Well, of course it had snowed, Madison thought, glancing out the window in their room. What was Stephanie making such a big fuss about?

Dad screamed, too. "I don't believe this! How on earth did *this* happen?"

Phin leaped off the bed and scampered into the other room when he heard Dad's booming voice. Madison and Aimee shot each other a look and then jumped out of their beds, curious. They raced into the living room.

It was quite a sight to behold.

There, in the center of the living-room carpet, was a big, white snowdrift. High above them, one of the skylights had opened, allowing snow to come in during the night.

"This will be our own personal ski trail, I guess," Stephanie joked.

King of the bad jokes, Dad chimed in: "Maybe we should call it Little Mountain."

Madison and Aimee looked straight at the two of them with their eyes bulging. How could they joke at a time like that?

"If we light a fire in the fireplace, will it melt faster?" Dad asked.

The four of them burst into laughter.

Stephanie dialed the main lodge, and immediately they were sent a cleaning crew, a technician, *and* a house manager. The manager insisted that the resort would reimburse them for one night's stay. He also said they'd pay for the Finn family's lift tickets *and* lunch that day at Big Mountain.

"These things just don't happen at Treetops," the manager said, apologizing again and again. "I give you my personal assurance that the rest of your stay will be problem free."

The manager stuck to his word. Within a half hour, the lodge was in perfect shape again, except for the chill resulting from the window's having been open most of the night. Shortly after the manager left, a Treetops chef (French, of course) personally delivered a cart with breakfast for all of them. Madison and Aimee oohed and aahed as they picked out their favorite treats.

"This place is like something out of the movies," Aimee said, pouring homemade granola into a bowl of berry yogurt. "My mom and dad would even eat here—and you know how picky they are."

Madison bit into a strawberry and then a warm chocolate croissant. "Dad, did I say thank you for taking us here?" she asked. "Thank you times a zillion."

"No thanks necessary, Maddie," Dad said. "Now that our chalet snowstorm has been cleared away, let's eat, get ready, and get over to Big Mountain for some real powder. I'm dying to hit those trails."

The four sat down to eat the rest of their breakfast. While Stephanie read the newspaper, Dad buttered his toast and peppered his eggs.

Everything was going great until Dad picked up a salt shaker and dumped the contents onto his breakfast plate. The pile of salt looked like a miniversion of the snowdrift that had just been cleared away in their living room.

"Wait! Spilled salt!" Madison cried. She leaned down to grab a pinch and threw it over her shoulder.

"Rwowwoowowowowowow!" Phin yelped.

"What are you doing, Madison?" Dad asked.

"Spilled salt is bad luck, Dad!" Madison exclaimed.

"Blinding your dog is pretty bad, too," Aimee said sarcastically.

Madison shot Aimee a look. She wanted to say something clever, but she didn't. Dad was getting impatient. He clapped his hands together and pushed the girls into the other room.

"Enough chaos!" Dad declared. "Let's get ready."

"Actually, Jeff, I think the girls should probably call home, right?" Stephanie suggested. "Aimee, why don't you check in with your mom? You, too, Maddie."

Aimee used Stephanie's cell phone first. Madison called home, too, but her mom was out. Then she dragged herself into the other room, having no idea what she would wear.

Aimee unzipped her suitcase and took out a perfectly matched outfit—a pair of purple ski pants and an orange fleece pullover. Underneath, she would wear a little shirt with flowers embroidered across the neckline.

"You have ski pants?" Madison asked. "But you hardly ever go skiing."

Aimee nodded. "I know, but these were on sale last winter."

Madison opened her suitcase and took a deep breath. First, she pulled out a pair of jeans, but Aimee tut-tutted her ("They're not waterproof, Maddie. You'll be soaked!") and made Madison put the jeans back into her bag.

"Jeans are for après-ski," Aimee said, trying to sound important and oh-so-French.

So Madison pulled out her lone pair of red snow pants. She hardly ever wore them, and they weren't exactly super fashionable, but they were warm and waterproof, and that was the main thing. Then, she pulled on a white turtleneck and a blue cardigan sweater.

"Maddie," Aimee said when she saw the outfit. "What is that? You'll look like the American flag."

"I will?" said Madison dumbly.

"Let me help you choose your outfit," Aimee insisted.

Madison and Aimee picked through both of their

suitcases until they came up with a combination of clothes that worked. Aimee matched Madison's red pants with her own black, long-sleeved T-shirt and turtleneck sweater. She also lent Madison a fun pink knitted hat. Aimee wore a skullcap decorated with flowers. After dressing, they rushed to meet Dad and Stephanie and get shuttle service to Big Mountain. The family dropped Phin off at the pet-sitting area in the main lodge; there he was joined by a fat Maltese, a yipping Yorkshire terrier, and a nervous-looking cat named Trix.

After the snowstorm the night before, the day was crisp and bright. The air smelled like wood smoke and pine trees. The foursome piled into the shuttle bus along with another family. One of the boys was kind of cute, Madison noticed. Aimee apparently thought so, too. She flirted with him all the way to the mountain.

They arrived and disembarked in front of the Big Mountain chalet. Inside the doors was the biggest fireplace Madison or Aimee had ever seen. People rushed around with hot drinks, ice skates, and skis. The line for lift tickets for one side of the mountain was halfway out the door.

Stephanie grabbed Madison by the shoulders and whispered in her ear. "I'm so glad we're here in one piece. I wasn't sure we'd make it."

Madison chuckled. "Me, neither."

Aimee seemed in awe of the outfits people were

wearing. "Maddie, you were so right," she said. "This is a major fashion scene. I am so glad we rethought your outfit."

Madison nodded. "Me, too," she said. But, what Madison was really thinking was, What am I doing here?

Dad learned where they could rent skis, ski boots, and other equipment. They headed for another building attached to the chalet. The line there was even longer than the one for lift tickets. Over the loudspeakers, announcements were being made about ski lessons and other events at the mountain.

Madison and Aimee wandered over to a giant map on one side of the room. It showed all of the ski trails at Big Mountain. The highest elevation was over 4,600 feet. It was a peak called Top Dog.

"That's high, isn't it?" Madison said as she looked up at the mountain through giant glass windows on one side of the room. "I can't really see the top. Is it foggy, or are those clouds?"

Aimee was too busy scoping out the other people in the room to reply to Madison's question. She grabbed Madison by the shoulders and whispered in her ear.

"Don't look now, but I think Hart is here," she said.

Madison felt her stomach flip-flop. Her knees wobbled. "Where?" she squeaked. "Hart's *here*?"

"Yeah, look over there. . . ." Aimee said as she pointed across the room.

Madison looked and saw an older, bald man wearing rainbow-colored suspenders. He struggled with the knotted laces on his ice skates. His face was flushed red from trying to pull off the skates.

"That's Hart in fifty years!" Aimee said.

"Very funny, Aim," Madison said, her lip curling in a sneer. "I thought you meant—oh, never mind what I thought."

Aimee smiled. "Maddie, I was only joking."

Madison was a little mad about being duped, but she faked a laugh. "Ha-ha."

Dad led the girls over to the information desk to sign up for their ski lessons. A big sign over the desk read: PEEWEESKI.

Madison and Aimee looked at each other and groaned. Then they saw the second sign, which read: TEENSKI. Under it, an instructor wearing huge sunglasses, a bronzy tan, and a plum-colored parka was filling out papers. He waved as people passed.

"Hello," Aimee said, walking right over to the man.

He looked up. "Yes? May I help you?" he said. His eyes were like melted caramels. He had a thick accent. Was it Spanish?

"We're here for lessons," Aimee said.

The bronze-skinned man smiled wide. "Are you?" he said. "Well, I'm the instructor."

Madison grabbed the table to steady herself. "Can we sign up for you?"

Aimee giggled. "She means, can we register for you *and* your lessons?"

"Certainly," the man said. "I'm Carlos. Let me get Jennifer. She will help get you signed up."

Madison had to grab Aimee's wrist to keep from toppling over onto one side. Carlos was a major babe. He left them both tongue-tied.

"I am heading back to the slopes, but I see you later, yes?" Carlos said.

Neither Aimee nor Madison could stop grinning.

"Yes," they said at exactly the same time, staring as Carlos walked away.

After Jennifer came by and took down their information, they prepared to meet Dad and Stephanie for a snack in the Big Mountain Diner. On the way, they stopped into one of the restrooms.

Madison stepped up to the sink and smiled at her reflection.

In the center of her two front teeth there was a something red. A piece of strawberry!

"Aim, how could you not tell me that I had food in my teeth?" Madison cried.

A woman in a fur-trimmed ski parka and matching boots gave Madison a funny look before walking out of the bathroom.

"I didn't see anything in your teeth, I swear," Aimee said.

Madison quickly picked out the bit of strawberry and sat down on a small, hard couch in the restroom waiting area.

"He must have seen it, though," Madison said.

Aimee giggled. "So what?" she said. "He's only the ski instructor, Maddie. Who cares?"

Madison shrugged. "I do. I care," she said, knowing that Aimee would have cared twice as much if she'd been the one caught with food in her teeth.

As they walked off to meet Dad at the restaurant, Madison tried not to obsess about what had happened, but it was hard to ignore her gut feeling. Just when something seemed right, bad luck came along.

Even though Aimee didn't believe in bad luck, Madison was convinced it had been following them around since the trip started.

Chapter 6

Madison and Aimee stood crushed up against the Big Mountain chalet wall for almost an hour as they waited to rent ski stuff. When they finally reached the front of the line, a redheaded woman in a pink ski suit asked them for their shoe sizes. She looked like a model from some ski magazine, her lips covered in shining gloss as she spoke to them. In fact, as far as Madison was concerned, half the people in the ski shop looked like models.

"Okay, girls," the pink lady said, "Do you have your parental permission slips?"

Dad and Stephanie had filled out all of the necessary paperwork so that Madison and Aimee could take lessons on their own.

"We'll keep your boots, skis, and poles here until your beginners' lesson this afternoon," the woman said as she handed them a yellow ticket. "Just bring this back and you can get everything you need. And don't forget! You'll have to read all the regulations for the slopes, girls. You are beginners, aren't you?"

"Yeah," Aimee said. "How can you tell?"

The woman laughed. "Good luck!" she said.

"Okay, let's see," Aimee said, reading one of the flyers. "In order to ski, we need sunblock, apparently. And a helmet, too. I think. I can't tell if it's required or what. But we need sunglasses and waterproof clothes and gloves and . . . Maddie, I have this stuff in my suitcase. Do you?"

Madison rolled her eyes. "Of course not," she said. "This trip is so complicated. I barely have clothes to wear away from the slopes, remember?"

"Oh, Maddie," Aimee said, wrapping her arm around Madison's shoulders. "You look great in whatever you wear."

Madison wanted to burst out laughing. Luckily for them, there was a ski-shop outlet on the Big Mountain property. And Stephanie was in the mood to shop. After lunch, Stephanie and Dad treated Madison to a pair of ultracool shades (with deep purple frames and mirrored lenses), a woolen headband, and a new pair of waterproof gloves (also in purple, because nothing seemed to come in Madison's favorite color, orange). But the best thing they bought for Madison was the perfect addition to her ski outfit—a pair of pants with a bib that fit over Madison's shirt. Aimee was jealous.

"You look like a real skier," Aimee said when Madison tried them on.

Madison beamed at herself in the mirror.

She really did look like a skier.

While Dad and Stephanie headed up the mountain for their own ski adventure, Madison and Aimee took their yellow tickets and went to retrieve their rented boots and skis. They needed to get ready for their two o'clock lesson.

The lessons were all held at the same place on the mountain, an area called Big Ski. As they approached on foot, Madison was nearly run over by a racing snowmobile—or at least it felt that way. Everyone was rushing to see someone or something. Aimee thought she saw lights flashing like a camera's.

"Excuse me," Madison asked an older gentleman standing on the sidelines in his ski goggles, with an annoyed look on his face. "What's going on?"

"Those movie stars think they own the place," the man said with a grunt. "Well, I was here first, I'll tell you. Been coming to this mountain for forty-nine years."

"Did he say *movie stars*?" Aimee asked. She grabbed Madison's elbow. "What are we standing here for? Let's go see who it is!"

Madison and Aimee scrambled across the snow and pushed their way through a throng of kids and adults. Somewhere along the way, they got separated.

"Aimee?" Madison called out. *"Aimee?"* By now, she could tell that the flashing lights definitely were those of paparazzi cameras. The crowd was too noisy for Aimee to hear Madison's cries.

Ooooooooof!

Madison was knocked to the ground by a young boy hurrying in the opposite direction. He extended his hand and helped her to her feet.

"Sorry," the boy said. "That was my fault."

Madison shook the snow off her butt and legs and regained her composure as best as she could. Aimee had not yet reappeared.

"Thanks," she said, as the boy retrieved Madison's new purple sunglasses from the snow.

"Are you okay? I really slammed into you," the boy said with a big smile.

Madison smiled right back. She wondered what the boy's name was.

"I'm Hugh," the boy said, as if he'd read her mind. "Hugh Jackson."

"Oh, hi. I'm Madison," she said. "Madison Finn."

Just then, Aimee caught up.

"You left me back there!" Aimee said, pretending to whine. She seemed not to notice the boy standing next to Madison. In fact, she blocked Madison's view of the boy altogether.

"Attention!" one of the Big Mountain ski employees yelled through a bullhorn. "Your attention, please! There is no lingering on the slopes. Please make your way to a lodge or trail. Thank you for your cooperation."

"Did you see him?" a girl screamed. "He's way cuter than on TV!"

"Who? *Who?*" Aimee asked. The girl didn't hear Aimee, so she knuckled her way into the crowd, dragging Madison along behind her. "Maddie, come on! We have to see who it is! Hurry!"

Madison looked back to smile at Hugh again, but he was gone.

They moved up past a few rows of people, and the star came into view.

"Oh, my God!" Aimee squealed. "It's Foster Lane! He's here! I can't believe this. Madison, this is the greatest day of my entire life. I—can't—breathe."

Madison laughed. She liked Foster Lane's looks. He was cute. He wasn't a very good actor, though. But Aimee didn't agree. She worshipped every little thing he did, from TV shows to music videos to some commercial for Bubblewad Gum.

Aimee's eyes widened till they looked like pie plates, and she batted her eyelashes the way she often did to get a boy's attention. Madison hung back a bit.

Foster, dressed in a cool blue ski suit and enormous ski goggles, waved to the crowd. He was getting ready to head over to the ski lift with his snowboard. Surrounding him was a group of friends (or were those bodyguards?); in a flash, he came and went, and once the crowd dispersed, the usual ebb and flow of activity resumed on the Big Mountain slopes.

Aimee stood there until Foster's ski lift began its ascent.

"I guess that was lucky," Madison said, "Seeing him here."

"Luck had nothing whatsoever to do with it," Aimee said. "These things just happen. I knew he'd be here. I knew it!"

Madison smiled at her BFF again. Sometimes Aimee could act so serious, and sometimes she acted downright silly. But that was what Madison liked best about Aimee. She was never afraid just to say what she was thinking. She was bold enough to run and try to shake the hand of her favorite TV star— even if she hadn't *this* time.

"It's too bad we got here late," Madison said, watching Foster and his entourage dangle in the lift high above the slopes. Cameras flashed up into the sky.

"Missed him? Not a chance!" Aimee cried. "I predict that I will meet Foster Lane and get his autograph before this week is through," she said.

"But you don't know if he'll be here for a week," Madison said.

"Then I'll get it sooner than that," Aimee said, sounding ultraconfident. "I will! Don't you believe me?"

Madison didn't know what to think or say. When Aimee set her mind to something, she was often successful. Maybe it was a combination of always speaking her mind and batting her eyelashes. Madison wasn't sure.

About a hundred yards away, they spotted Carlos again. He stood before a group of skiers dressed in a rainbow of ski gear. Madison and Aimee moved toward him. Their pickup and drop-off spot was toward the side.

Madison's ski boots were a perfect fit. She felt like a real pro wearing them. But the rest of the equipment was a bit of a mystery. She looked at the bindings on her skis and wondered how she would ever lock them on to her boots and actually ski down Big Mountain. And what were the poles for? Every time she tried to poke one of them into the snow, she nearly tripped.

Aimee had trouble getting her gear on, too. But soon they were both suited up and trudging over to Carlo's area, skis and poles in hand.

"Hello, again," a voice said to Madison.

Madison turned to see the boy she'd just met a few moments before, Hugh. This time she stared at his face and took it all in. He had a row of freckles across his nose and cheeks. His eyes were deep green.

His hair was sandy colored—at least the bangs that she saw poking out from under his bright blue hat.

Mmmm. He was cute.

"Hello to you," Madison said, feeling a warm blush spreading across her cheeks.

"Yeah, hello," Aimee said, leaning in. "Are you here for the ski lessons, too?"

Madison looked down at her feet, which seemed twice their normal size in the bulky ski boots. There was no running away from this. She looked back up at Hugh and did something she'd only done a few times before. She batted her eyelashes.

Hugh looked away with a grin.

Was he blushing, too, or was it the cold air that was making him turn pink?

Aimee didn't have a chance to say anything more. Carlos clapped his hands and started the first lesson.

There were a total of eleven kids, including Madison and Aimee. The group would meet for three days, at which point, Carlos promised, every beginning skier would be able to walk in skis and to start, stop, and get on the ski lift unassisted.

"That's it?" Aimee said, sounding disappointed.

Madison nudged her friend. "That's more than what we know now, right?" she said. "Why do you have to say something about everything? Shhh!"

Aimee pretended to zip up her lips. And she did stop talking. But she couldn't keep still. Off the slopes, Aimee was always in the kind of constant motion that went with being a dancer. On skis, that motion turned into a sequence of jumps and starts that made it seem as though she were having some kind of nervous fit.

Madison tried to focus on the instructor. At first she listened to all of the words he said, but then she started to dissect his face, his outfit, and his whole look. Would he make a good male model? Was he cuter than Foster Lane? Was he cuter than Hart Jones?

Maybe.

Carlos had applied a glob of white sunblock to his nose, but it didn't look goofy at all. On Carlos, a glob of sunblock looked positively cool.

"Maddie," Aimee said after a few minutes. "What's up with that guy back there in the black parka?"

"Um . . ." Madison said, catching her breath. "Who?"

Aimee snorted. "That guy we just saw!"

"I don't know who you're talking about," Madison said.

"Maddie, you are such a bad liar," Aimee said with a grin.

Madison let out a little laugh. "He's cute, right?" she said.

Carlos had obviously heard the chatter. He stopped speaking and turned toward Madison and Aimee.

"Excuse me, ladies," he said in his stilted accent. "In order to ski, you need to pay attention."

Madison gulped. All eyes had turned toward them. Even Hugh was staring.

Aimee and Madison quickly promised to be quiet. Carlos continued with the lesson. As he spoke, Madison scanned the crowd. Everyone seemed to be listening intently. The group consisted mostly of teens, Madison noticed. She and Aimee were on the younger end of the spectrum. At least everyone was a beginner, so Madison hoped she wouldn't stick out much.

"This is the rule," Carlos said. He looked right at Madison. "You must be serious about your skiing if you want to be safe."

Carlos pointed to a very big chart concerning skier etiquette. The code of rules and behavior was printed in bold black letters.

1. Always stay in control. Make sure you are able to stop or avoid other people or objects.
2. People ahead of you have the right of way. You must avoid them.
3. Observe all posted signs and warnings. Keep off closed trails and out of closed areas.
4. Prior to using any lift, you must have the knowledge and ability to load, ride, and unload safely.
5. Respect Big Mountain. Do not litter or use bad language.

Madison glanced over at Hugh to see if he was looking in her direction, but he wasn't. He was sliding his left boot in and out of his left ski binding.

"Maddie!" Aimee whispered. "How old do you think Carlos is?"

"Older than Ben Buckley," Madison teased. "Like, as old as your dad, probably."

Aimee gave Madison a playful shove. "He is *not*!"

"Aim, I'm twelve. You're thirteen. Remember?"

"Sometimes I wish I were eighteen," Aimee said with a sigh. "It seems like forever until we're old enough to really do anything fun. Doesn't it?"

"Eighteen? What are you talking about?" Madison said. Of course, Madison knew what Aimee meant. Lately her BFF had mentioned wanting to attend a few ninth-grade parties. Aimee sometimes wanted to go places that her older brothers went, even though her parents would never allow it.

"I've decided I'm going to have a double crush, on Carlos and Foster Lane, on this ski trip," Aimee declared. "And you can crush on the black-parka guy. How does that sound?"

"Shhh!" Madison said, as if Hugh could have heard. "It sounds crazy, Aim. What about Ben?" she asked.

"I can like more than one person at once, can't I?" Aimee said, readjusting her hat and gloves. "Of course, I still like Ben—when we're at school. But here, things are different. This is vacation. You're allowed to have separate vacation crushes."

Carlos shot the girls another glare and they stopped talking for good. It was time to start paying attention if they wanted to learn anything about skiing.

Aimee thought they'd take off down the mountain right away, but an hour into the lesson, the only thing Carlos had shown them how to do was walk in their skis. Madison was proud of the fact that she'd fallen only six times and only when'd she tried to lift instead of slide. Of course, lucky Aimee hadn't fallen at all. That impressed Carlos. He came over and complimented Aimee on her balance at least three times. Madison was counting. She wondered why she couldn't be the teacher's pet for once.

By the time Carlos got around to demonstrating the "wedge" stance, Madison maneuvered to stand near Hugh. But Hugh didn't seem to notice. He continued to struggle with boots that kept coming out of their bindings. Eventually, Hugh's ski boots let out a loud *snap*. Madison wanted to see what was happening and talk to him, but just as she got closer, Carlos whisked him away to get the broken ski fixed.

"Hey, Maddie, look at me! Look at meeeeeee!" Aimee said, demonstrating her skill with the wedge.

Madison turned to look at Aimee without sliding and lost her balance.

Thunk.

"Are you okay?" Aimee said as she gracefully glided over.

Madison groaned. Her butt ached from the fall. Would her entire side be bruised now? How embarrassing!

As the first group lesson ended, Aimee was just getting into it, but Madison was ready to get off Big Mountain—in a big way. The temperature was dropping as the sun sank in the sky, and Madison's fingertips were cold, even under her brand-new gloves. She didn't feel like falling anymore. Her backside couldn't take it. Her ego couldn't, either.

Carlos helped Madison and Aimee to remove their skis and boots and return them, with the poles, to a storage area near the place where they'd taken the lesson. For the next few lessons, they would keep their equipment there rather than dragging it back to the rental area or to where they were staying.

As the ski group dispersed—and Hugh did not reappear, much to Madison's disappointment—they headed back to the main lodge to meet up with Stephanie and Dad.

"So? How was the lesson?" Dad bellowed when he saw Madison and Aimee walking toward him. "Ready for the black-diamond slopes yet?"

Madison knew that the black-diamond trail was the hardest one in the entire complex.

"We can do that, right, Maddie?' Aimee chirped. She made whooshing noises and motioned as though she were headed down a super-size slope.

Madison groaned. "I'm still working on just *standing* in the skis, Dad."

"You'll get there," Stephanie said, always supportive.

"Did you have fun today?" Madison asked her dad.

"I'm a little rusty," Dad said, cracking his knuckles dramatically.

Stephanie threw her arm around him. "You are a terrific skier, Jeff," she said. "You just need a whole mountain to yourself."

Aimee and Madison laughed. "What happened?" they asked.

"Oh," Dad sighed. "I knocked over part of a barrier on the side."

"And nearly collided with a family of four!" Stephanie added. "Luckily, there were no major injuries."

"There were no injuries at all!" Dad clucked. He winked at Madison. "I'm saving my big tricks for tomorrow."

As they headed toward Treetops on the shuttle bus, Dad produced a small blue box in each hand. He gave one to Madison and one to Aimee.

Aimee squealed. "A present? Are you kidding?"

"Daddy! Thank you," Madison said. She opened her box. Inside was a silver bunny charm on a chain. Aimee had gotten the same thing.

"They're lucky charms for our two special ski bunnies," explained Stephanie. "Maybe they will bring you extra luck over the vacation."

Madison knew Aimee wasn't as keen on luck or lucky charms as she was, but Aimee seemed happy to get a cool new necklace. Aimee threw her arms around Stephanie and then Dad, planting a kiss on his cheek.

"Thanks," Aimee gushed.

Madison held the charm necklace tightly in her hand. It shimmered. It felt warm. It was lucky. She knew it.

Despite a day of pratfalls in the snow, Madison Finn remained determined to have a lucky week.

A silver rabbit would make it all possible.

Chapter 7

Lucky Charm

Rude Awakening: You're no bunny until some bunny loves you. LOL.

I love my new ski bunny necklace.

I just hope it works.

Been thinking about all the bad omens we had coming up to the mountain. And who has snow fall in the middle of the living room? Maybe this lucky charm can arm me against bad luck once and for all. I will still cross my fingers and keep an eye out for black cats, too, of course. Aimee says I'm crazy. She makes fun of all my superstitions. When she put her new necklace in a drawer, I asked her how she could do that, and she

81

said, "Because it doesn't really match my shirt." Can you imagine?! She just doesn't get it.

We're about to go out for our first big dinner here at the resort. I hope they don't serve goose liver or snails. I remember going to a party for the film editing crew Mom works with at Budge Films when they served this fancy mystery food. I ate octopus without realizing it!

I'd better go. It's getting late. Aimee's wearing the nicest sweater set and those embroidered pants that look so good on her. As usual, I'm outfit-less. Grrrr. Will the power of the bunny charm help me?

Stephanie poked her head into Madison and Aimee's room. "Are you girls dressed yet?" she asked.

Stephanie wore a long black flowing skirt and a snug white blouse with a gold-beaded choker. Her hair was piled on top of her head and fixed with gold combs.

Aimee stood up. "You look so pretty," she told Stephanie.

"Aw, this little old thing?" Stephanie said, affecting modesty. She admired Aimee's outfit aloud. "I like those pants, Aimee. Is that a butterfly pattern?"

"These are my *favorite* dressy pants," Aimee said. "Do you think they're dressy enough?"

Stephanie nodded. "And what about you,

Maddie?" she asked.

Madison didn't respond. She just snapped her laptop shut. Meanwhile, Phin (who had been retrieved earlier from the pet-sitting center) jumped up from his large plaid dog pillow. He let out a howl.

"See? Even Phinnie knows I have nothing to wear," Madison said.

"Come on, there has to be something in your suitcase," Stephanie said, rubbing Madison's shoulder. "Let's take a look together."

"I've already gone through the suitcase three times. There is nothing that I would want to wear to a fancy restaurant," Madison said. "I barely scraped together enough clothes to wear on the slopes. Let's face it. I am seriously fashion-challenged this week."

"Maddie!" Aimee cried. "Quit freaking out. You have plenty of cute clothes. We went over the list on the phone before we left. I told you that you look good in anything. I don't know why you don't believe me."

"I believe you, Aim," Madison explained. "It's just that my clothes don't."

Stephanie wrinkled her brow and leaned over Madison's open suitcase. With Stephanie's and Aimee's help, Madison decided upon a short corduroy skirt and a long-sleeved shirt with flower buttons. She pulled on ribbed brown tights to go underneath and unbuttoned the top two buttons of her shirt so that her lucky bunny charm necklace was visible. She couldn't risk anything blocking her lucky vibes.

The Treetops restaurant was mobbed. During their twenty-two-minute wait for a table, Aimee and Dad wandered off to look at an art exhibit in a small gallery that was situated beside the restaurant. Madison and Stephanie eventually followed.

"Stephanie," Madison asked cautiously. "I have a serious question. Will you give me a serious answer?"

"Gee, Maddie, it sounds like you have something on your mind," Stephanie said.

"Do you believe in superstitions?" Madison asked.

"Oh! Well, sure," Stephanie replied easily. "My mother used to have this one superstition about sneezing. Let's see. The number of sneezes means something. So it's one for sorrow; two for joy; three for a letter; four for a boy; five for silver; six for gold; seven for a secret, never to be told."

"'Four sneezes for a boy'?" Madison said. "Then next time I sneeze I'm going to do it four times on purpose."

Stephanie laughed.

"What are you two up to? Do you like the paintings?" Dad asked, circling back toward Madison and Stephanie. He gave Stephanie a kiss.

Madison left her dad and stepmother alone and shuffled over to Aimee, who stood in front of a portrait of a ballerina.

"That looks like you," Madison said.

"I wish," Aimee said. "Too bad I'm not a real ballerina."

"Of course you're real!" Madison said. "You're the best ballerina I know."

"Thanks, Maddie," Aimee said with a wide grin. The pair locked arms and walked around, giggling, as they surveyed the rest of the pictures in the gallery. It actually took ten extra minutes before their table was ready and they went back into the dining room with Dad and Stephanie.

The fancy dinner was snail free, much to Madison's relief. There were a few odd items on the menu, like buffalo quesadillas and grouper with pomegranate sauce, but it was mostly food Madison and Aimee liked and were willing to taste. After the main course, Dad ordered a special chocolate soufflé that the four of them shared. Outside the window by their table, it appeared to be snowing again. They sat there and ate dessert, watching the snow fall.

"I love this weather," Stephanie said. "It's so . . . cozy."

The waiter came by and delivered coffee and cookies, compliments of Treetops. "It's a real blizzard lockdown tonight," the waiter said. "Keep an eye out for Mr. White."

"Who's he?" Madison asked.

The waiter explained that a long time ago an

older man named Mr. White, who was staying at the resort, had gotten lost on the way to his chalet and spent the night outside alone, face down in the snow. The storm had buried him, and he was not found until spring. Supposedly his ghost remained on the property, and whenever it snowed a lot, he came back to haunt places on the property like the main lodge, his old room, and the skating chalet.

"A snow ghost? Get out!" Aimee said. "That is just something you made up to scare us."

"Hey, I couldn't make up something that good," the waiter said as he cleared away a few more of the dishes.

"Where's Mr. White's old room?" Madison asked nervously.

"I think it was at Eagle's Nest," the waiter replied.

Madison nearly dropped her fork. "That's *our* cabin!" she cried.

"Gee," the waiter said. "Maybe I should wrap up an extra slice of the soufflé for the ghost?" He chuckled and winked.

Dad and Stephanie smiled as the waiter dropped the check on the table and walked away, carrying some empty plates.

Aimee started to laugh out loud.

"Wait. What's so funny? It's not funny," Madison said.

"Sure it is. A ghost? Maddie, have you lost it?" Aimee asked. "The waiter is goofing around. He almost had me for a minute. . . ."

"How do you know it isn't real?" Madison said. "I believe in that stuff."

"But you believe in chain letters, too," Aimee said.

"You're not superstitious, Aimee?" Stephanie asked. She seemed to sense that the conversation was heating up a little bit.

"I'm not really superstitious," Aimee shrugged. "Not like Maddie. I just don't see the point," she said.

Madison absentmindedly touched her rabbit charm.

"Well, I imagine a snowstorm up here means some serious snow," Dad said, briskly changing the subject.

"Hey, Mr. Finn?" Aimee asked. "Do you remember the time when we were all over at your house in Far Hills, and it snowed for three days, and the plow came down the street and almost buried me and Maddie in a pile of snow?"

"Oh, yes," Dad said. "I remember."

"And remember, Mrs. Finn had to call the police?" Aimee went on.

Dad smiled and shook his head. "Yup. Fran would never let me live that one down. 'How could you let the girls play by the sidewalk?' she said to me."

Aimee started to laugh. "Remember that, Maddie? Your mom was standing there on the sidewalk digging us out with her bare hands, and it was so cold, and we were stuck."

"Fran said that I'd turned you both into snow-girls," Dad chuckled.

Madison laughed, too.

"Would you three excuse me for a moment?" Stephanie said all of a sudden. She pushed her chair out and turned for the ladies' room.

"Everything okay, Steph?" Dad called out.

Stephanie turned back and mouthed the words *I'm fine*.

"We were talking about Mom a lot, weren't we?" Madison squirmed in her seat. "Aimee, why did you keep bringing her up?"

"Huh? Me?" Aimee said. "I was just . . . well . . . sorry, I didn't know it was a bad thing to talk about your mom."

"It isn't a bad thing," Dad said. He shot a look at Madison.

"Don't look at me like that, Dad," Madison said. "It's totally weird to talk about Mom in front of Stepmom and you know it."

"Maddie, Stephanie is fine with it," Dad said. "She likes your mother."

"Whatever," Madison said. She glared at Aimee.

"Maddie, what is wrong? Are you blaming me for Stephanie getting up and leaving?" Aimee said. "Because I think that is totally unfair—"

"And I think that you—" Madison was cut off by

Dad's loud voice.

"Wait a minute. Girls, *girls*," Dad said sternly.

Madison and Aimee both shrank down into their seats.

The funny thing about having Aimee on a family vacation was that sometimes she fit in too well. Sometimes she was like Madison's surrogate sister. She ranked way higher than a BFF, anyway. After all, they had been friends since they were born.

Dad lectured Madison and Aimee both about behaving themselves on the trip. Madison felt as though she were in first grade—not seventh—when he talked to her that way, but she tried really hard not to pout.

A few silent moments later, Stephanie returned to the table. Still, one was saying anything. Stephanie looked around the table with a concerned look on her face.

"Did I miss something?" she asked, taking a big spoonful of soufflé. "Who died?"

"I'm sorry!" Aimee blurted. "It's all my fault."

"Your fault for what?" Stephanie said. "What's going on here, Jeff?"

Madison spoke up instead of Dad. "We never should have mentioned Mom, Stephanie. We're sorry."

Stephanie bowed her head and smiled. "Girls," she said slowly. "You can talk about Madison's mom. She's a part of our lives."

Madison gulped. "I know, but—"

"No buts," Stephanie said.

Dad patted the edge of the table. "Look, ladies, why don't we change the subject?" Dad suggested.

No one said anything.

"Aimee, you start," Dad said. "Change the subject."

"Oh," Aimee said, dipping her spoon into her serving of soufflé. "Let's see . . . I hope we can ski somewhere tomorrow. I mean, we are on a mountain, and I'd like to go somewhere, right? Hey, Madison, maybe you and the black-parka guy will ski together tomorrow."

"Aimee!" Madison said angrily. She kicked Aimee under the table, but missed and kicked the table leg instead.

"What was that?" Stephanie said, glancing under the table, which was now shaking a little.

Madison looked around. She was feeling too self-conscious even to lean down and grab her knee. "What was what?"

"Who's this 'black-parka guy'?" Dad asked with a grimace.

Before Madison was forced to say anything, Stephanie stood up and suggested that they go for a walk on the grounds behind the restaurant.

The paths were clear of snow, and the moon lit up the grounds. A surprising number of people were going for short strolls after dinner.

Although it was very, very, *very* cold outside, Madison was happy to be there. She needed to cool down after the flare-up with Aimee.

Up in the sky, stars glimmered. Madison wished it were summer instead of winter so she could crash down onto the ground and stare at this light show. But falling to the ground now meant freezing her behind. She did not feel like turning into an ice cube. There was plenty of time for that on the ski slopes tomorrow.

When they returned to Eagle's Nest, everyone said their hellos to Phin and then headed for their rooms. Madison was distressed to see clothes lying everywhere—leftovers from her fashion emergency earlier in the evening, a disaster from which she'd successfully recovered.

Aimee helped her to pick up and reorganize. After a while, they both got sleepy and got into their pajamas. Although they'd crawled under the covers, Madison pulled out her laptop. She opened a new file and started to type. Aimee fell asleep within a few minutes.

Hoo-hooooooo.

Madison jumped. What was that? After a few moments, she continued typing again.

Hoo-hooooooo.

Madison jumped out of the bed, clasping her computer. "Aimee!" she cried.

"What? What is it?" Aimee asked, jumping out of bed.

Madison didn't have to answer. The owl

91

answered for her.

Hoo-hooooooo.

"Oh, no! Three times! Bad luck!" Madison shouted.

"Huh? Three what?" Aimee asked, rubbing her eyes. "Maddie, stop obsessing about your stupid superstitions."

"What do you mean, *stupid*?" Madison asked.

"I mean, can you please stop being so neurotic for five minutes and just go back to sleep?"

Madison caught her breath. This was her best friend. She didn't want to get mad. But she couldn't help herself.

"Neurotic? Quit acting like you know everything," Madison blurted out. She wished she could take it back the moment she had said it, but it was too late.

"What do you mean by that?" Aimee asked. "I don't know everything. Who said I knew everything?"

"Well, sometimes it seems like you always know everything," Madison said. "What's so wrong with my being superstitious?"

"It's just so . . . I don't know . . . so fake," Aimee said. "Do you really think crossing your fingers matters?"

Madison's jaw dropped. "I don't know. Why do you have to be mean about it? I don't make fun of all your dance stuff."

"What about my dance stuff?" Aimee asked

defensively.

"It's all you ever talk about," Madison said.

"That's not true," Aimee said. "Don't be mean."

"I'm not being mean!" Madison said.

"Wait, Maddie, I'm not being mean, either," Aimee said. "I'm being honest. You're my BFF, right? Aren't BFFs supposed to be honest?"

Madison didn't answer that one.

Aimee didn't ask the question twice.

Madison swallowed hard. She'd spent a zillion sleepovers with Aimee back in Far Hills and they'd never gotten into a fight.

At least, not like this one.

"Good night, Maddie," Aimee said, getting into bed again and rolling over onto her pillow.

"Good night," Madison said. She got back in bed and rolled over, too.

Under the covers again, Madison made a wish that she and Aimee would be back to normal the next day.

But without Aimee's knowing it, she crossed her fingers *and* her toes, just to be sure.

Chapter 8

Madison could hear everyone moving around inside the chalet, but she stayed buried under the blankets. She felt something hard up by her head. Ouch! She'd left her laptop on the bed after the fight with Aimee.

Laughter was coming from the next room. Madison could tell it was Aimee and Stephanie. She crawled out of bed and peered through the doorway.

Everyone was up. Stephanie was already dressed. Aimee was still in her floral pajamas with lace around the edges. Madison stood there in ripped sweatpants (again) and a tie-dyed T-shirt.

"Morning," Madison grumbled.

Phin scooted right over to say his good morning. He'd spent the night in the doggy bed that Dad had moved out by the living room sofa. Normally, Phin wouldn't sleep anywhere but right next to Madison, but for some reason he liked the Treetops doggy bed. Stephanie said it was because the bed had a down-filled pillow cover and a heating coil inside.

"What's up?" Aimee called out in a perky voice.

"Hey," Madison said. She was confused. Aimee was acting as if nothing had happened the night before. "How long have you been up?" Madison asked.

"An hour," Aimee said. "Stephanie and I were just hanging out."

"Aimee told me that you two had a big talk yesterday," Stephanie said.

Madison frowned. *A big talk?* What was that supposed to mean? Had Aimee told Stephanie about their fight?

"Aimee told me you had made a pact to get on the ski lift together this week," Stephanie said. "I think that is very ambitious—and exciting. Best friends trying new things together."

"Uh-huh," Madison said, blinking and acting as if any of it were something she'd heard before. "Well, that's us. Ambitious and exciting."

"We should hurry up and get dressed, Maddie, so we can hit the slopes for our lesson," Aimee said.

"After all, Carlos and the black-parka guy are waiting!"

"His name is Hugh," Madison said.

Stephanie rolled her eyes and chuckled. "My goodness. You girls are really boy crazy."

"You said you were once boy crazy, too!" Aimee cried.

Aimee and Stephanie laughed again, as if they were sharing a private joke.

Madison wanted in. After all, Stephanie was *her* stepmother. "What's so funny?" she asked.

"Before you woke up I was just telling Aimee about this guy I liked when I was about thirteen in Texas," Stephanie said. "I was mad for him and his cute dimples, even though he was fifteen. Crushes can be powerful motivators. I followed him everywhere. Of course, he wanted nothing to do with me."

"Oh," Madison said. She clutched at her chest. It ached.

Why was Stephanie sharing that story with Aimee before she shared it with Madison? Did jealousy really feel like—heartburn? Or was Madison just feeling leftover grumpiness from the previous night's fight with Aimee? And why did Aimee seem happy—not grumpy at all?

"Maddie?" Stephanie asked. "What is that on your face?"

Madison reached up to feel her face. She was afraid Stephanie was talking about Madison's facial

96

expression, and that it might have revealed her innermost thoughts.

"What's on my face?" Madison repeated.

"Yeah," Aimee added. "What *is* that?"

"Huh? What's wrong?" Madison asked, panicked. She went to look in the mirror on the living-room wall.

On Madison's left cheek was a deep red mark. Upon closer inspection, Madison realized it was the imprint of a bunny. She must have fallen asleep on top of her lucky necklace. Madison rubbed her cheek as hard as she could. By the time she stopped rubbing, the bunny outline was no longer visible. She hoped the redness would fade by the time the ski lesson began.

Some lucky charm.

"Maybe I should take this off," Madison said, fingering the charm.

"Why?" Aimee started to say. "It's cute, and I think—"

"I know what you think," Madison said, cutting Aimee off. She unhinged the necklace and placed it into its little box. "Don't obsess. Don't get all neurotic. I won't wear it. Okay, Aim?"

"Maddie, I was only . . ." Aimee's voice trailed off. "Do whatever you want. I'm not wearing mine, either. It's really no big deal."

Madison took a deep breath. Was she overreacting? Her gut told her that she should wear the charm. After all, it was a special gift from Dad. It was meant to help Madison become a genuine snow bunny.

But she didn't wear it. She put it on top of the dresser.

Aimee took forever to get dressed for their second day on the slopes, picking through her suitcase, wondering aloud what Carlos's favorite color and style were. She put her hair up and then took it down again three times before deciding upon the right do.

While she waited for Aimee to get ready, an impatient Madison opened her laptop to send an e-mail to Bigwheels. She had promised to write to her keypal once the vacation officially started. This was as good a time as any.

Madison clicked on NEW MESSAGE and started to type.

From: MadFinn
To: Bigwheels
Subject: Life in the Snow Lane
Date: Mon 1 Mar 9:14 AM
Where are you right now?

I'm up on a mountain in the middle of Nowheresville, in the middle of a sort-of fight with Aim and did I mention that there's a lot of snow up here?

Ur superstitious like me and that means u understand the way I think, right? So if someone gives you a lucky charm, what would u do? You don't put it in a drawer, right? Well, my BFF DID!

When this week started I thought that Aimee was the best person on the planet to go on a trip with me. But all of a sudden it's like she's CHANGED. Well, not changed. She's just not acting the way I wish she would act. She's really, really flirty this week for some reason and I don't know why. She keeps talking about guys that are so much older than us. It's so weird. Do ur friends ever go for older guys? Have any of ur BFFs ever turned into Dr. Jekyll and Miss Hyde right before ur very eyes? HELP MEEEEEE!

Yours till the bunny rabbits,

Maddie

p.s.: I'm learning how to get on a ski lift this week. WML.

p.p.s.: I think I may have met a QT

in our ski class. Yes, I really am trying to 4get about Hart. I'll write more 18r about him. :>)

"Hey, what are you writing?" Aimee asked, leaning over toward Madison's laptop.

Madison hit SEND so the Bigwheels message would disappear into cyberspace. She didn't want Aimee to see it.

"Is that an e-mail to your keypal?" Aimee asked.

"Yes," Madison said. At first, she had tried to keep Bigwheels a secret from her BFFs at school, but that hadn't lasted long. It was too hard to keep interesting facts from friends—and Bigwheels was definitely interesting.

"Cool. Well, I think I'm ready to go now," Aimee said. "Are you ready? You look nice today, Maddie. I think you're getting the hang of this ski fashion thing."

"You do?" Madison said. She smiled. A compliment about her clothes was enough to make Madison forgive and forget any moments of conflict she'd had with Aimee in the past twenty-four hours—sort of.

"Before we go, should we send Fiona an e-mail?" Madison asked.

Aimee sat down next to Madison and the laptop. "Totally!" she said. "Can I write it? We can send a copy to my e-mail address, too."

Madison clicked REPLY, but then Aimee took over.

```
From: MadFinn
To: Wetwinz; BalletGrl
Subject: Ski Bunnies
Date: Mon 1 Mar 9:56 AM
]--8 Hello California how are
you????? This is Madison and Aimee
writing you @ the same exact time
AGAIN. Ok, well it's Aimee writing
this time Maddie let me on her
laptop can u believe it? This place
is SOOOOO gorgeous and
```

"Hey, you two!" Dad called out. He poked his head into their room. "Maddie, can't you put down that laptop for one vacation? Stephanie and I have been sitting out here waiting for you girls to get ready."

"My bad, Mr. Finn," Aimee said. "Madison said we had to go, but I wanted to send an e-mail."

Dad rubbed his chin. "Well," he said. "Let's get moving now."

"Thanks," Madison whispered to Aimee as Dad ducked out.

Aimee grinned and took Madison's arm. "Like you wouldn't do that for me?" she asked matter-of-factly.

Madison didn't know what to say to that.

The pair helped Dad and Stephanie load up the Jeep with ski equipment (and Phinnie, too). The car was super packed, and so they were super squished in the backseat again. Plus, it had snowed more during the night. The light dusting made the roads extra slippery en route to Big Mountain.

Dad and Stephanie dropped Phin off at the pet-sitter's and then headed to the more difficult ski slopes for the day. Madison and Aimee went back to Carlos's ski lessons. The group from the day before had reassembled. Aimee and Madison picked up their equipment, joined by a bunch of other kids who had rented materials.

Carlos started off the lesson with a demonstration of Helmet Patrol, a program designed to get kids wearing helmets on the slopes. He explained that they wouldn't need the helmets for their lessons, but that once the skiing got more advanced, he would be recommending them.

"He looks even cuter today," Aimee whispered.

Madison tried to ignore Aimee. She didn't feel like talking about boys all the time—and she didn't want to get into trouble for gabbing during the presentation.

"Maddie, did you hear me?" Aimee said.

"Shhh!" Madison said. "We should listen."

"You're no fun," Aimee said. She rolled her eyes and stuck her poles in the snow with an annoyed little grunt.

Madison tried to ignore that, too. She scanned the crowd of participants for a black parka, but Hugh was not there.

The group spent the morning trying to climb a baby hill. They began at the bottom, each new skier clumsily trying to maneuver sideways without crashing into someone else. Carlos explained the difference between uphill and downhill skiing but Madison kept getting mixed up.

Aimee fell down for the first time in the soft, powdery snow when she tried the climb, and Madison burst out laughing.

"How can you laugh?" Aimee said, lying in the snow. "I'm stuck."

Madison crossed ski over ski and continued her own climb. She didn't need to rescue her friend, because two different boys in the group were already helping her. Carlos rushed over, too.

Time passed quicker than quickly on the ski slopes. After a bit of climbing and sliding back down, Madison started to feel a little woozy. The heat of the sun was going right for her nose. Sunblock! Madison had forgotten to wear any. She headed back to the equipment shed.

Ski over ski, Madison told herself as she walked slowly back. Every ounce of her being was saying, *DO NOT FALL.* That was only one of the ski mantras she'd adopted in the past twenty-four hours.

"Do not fall," she repeated aloud.

Madison found a tube of Burn Be Gone and smeared it on her nose.

"That's a good look for you," someone said from behind her.

It was Hugh. He had the same smear of white on his nose.

"Hi," Madison asked. "I didn't see you on the slopes when the lesson started. Were you there?"

"I had to go to this breakfast thing with my dad," Hugh explained. "I asked permission to come late to the lesson. How is it?"

"Fine," Madison said.

"Nice nose," Hugh said, indicating the sunblock. His voice had a lilt in it, and Madison smiled. Hugh was definitely crushworthy.

"Yeah, this is the new look," Madison said, touching her white nose. "So, are you going back to the lesson now?"

Hugh nodded. "If I don't fall first," he said.

Madison smiled, and they walked on together, ski over ski.

Aimee was still holding center stage back at the lesson. Carlos had Aimee stand up in front of the other group members to demonstrate a stopping technique. She waved her arms in the air, showing off.

"That's your friend, right?" Hugh asked. "She looks happy."

Madison nodded. "She's having a good time."

"Those are my friends over there," Hugh said, pointing across the snow. "Philip, Wick, and Roger."

"Wick?" Madison asked. A few yards away from where they were taking the beginner's ski lesson, a cluster of guys and girls lined up for the ski lift. They had apparently signed up for advanced ski lessons.

"Wick is short for 'wicked good skier,'" Hugh joked. "All my friends have been skiing forever, but I never did. I skate, though. I'm on my school hockey team."

Madison stared at Hugh's mouth while he talked. He played hockey, just like Hart.

"Where do you live?" Madison asked.

"We live in Reston, New York. It's a small town north of—"

"Far Hills," Madison interrupted. "You're kidding, right? I live in Far Hills."

"Whoa."

They glided over and lined up in front of Carlos, who had moved on to a new topic.

In the distance, Madison could hear the fast *swoosh* of a thousand skis dancing down Big Mountain.

At least she thought it was the sound of skiers.

It might have been her racing pulse.

Chapter 9

By midday, Madison and Aimee were feeling more in control of their skis—and their crushes. When she wasn't attempting to balance herself on her skis, Madison was busy figuring out new ways to get closer to Hugh.

Aimee was sticking close to Carlos, of course.

"The key to skiing is to master your equipment and your speed. If you feel yourself start to lose control, fall onto your backside or your side, and don't attempt to get up until you stop sliding," Carlos explained.

Madison snickered. "Fall on my butt? That's no problem for me."

"Me, neither," Hugh laughed.

"The easiest way to get hurt while skiing is to try

a run or a move that is too hard," Carlos went on. "Never attempt a jumping move or other trick unless you are being taught by an instructor."

Carlos led the group over to a large billboard with a map of the entire Big Mountain area and pointed out the easy and difficult slopes.

Madison noticed a trail marked Bad Luck Gully. She gulped.

Bad luck?

"Got any questions?" Carlos asked when he saw Madison's face. "You look a little worried. No worries, okay?"

Madison smiled. "Okay," she said softly.

Carlos clapped his hands. "Now, I need a volunteer for another demonstration," he said.

Aimee and Madison thrust their hands into the air at the same moment.

"I'll do it," they each said.

But Carlos looked in the opposite direction and called on someone else in the group, a girl named Beth. Carlos walked over and arranged Beth's body in the proper skiing position.

"Oh, that's great," Aimee huffed. "She didn't even volunteer."

"What's the big deal?" Madison asked.

"What do you mean, 'what's the big deal'? You raised your hand, too."

"Yeah, but . . ." Madison thought for a moment. "Forget it."

107

"Why are you acting so strange?" Aimee asked.

"Me? You're the one who's acting a little strange lately, Aimee. You remind me of . . . oh, I won't say it."

"Who?" Aimee asked.

Madison raised her fingers to her face and pretended to zip her lips.

"Who?" Aimee asked. "Tell me."

"You're acting like Poison Ivy would act," Madison said.

"What?" Aimee said. "You think I'm acting like the enemy?"

"No . . . of course not . . . oh . . . I don't know," Madison said, unsure about how to respond. She wanted to say, *Look, Aim, you* are *acting like Ivy and you can't deny it. You can't always hog Carlos, you know. You're not the center of the universe, you know.*

But that was the very last thing that Madison would ever have said out loud.

Carlos clapped his hands together again.

"I want you to try leaning on one ski," Carlos said. "It is the best way to get ahold of your balance."

Aimee tried putting all of her weight onto one ski. She got wobbly right away. Madison reached out and grabbed Aimee's parka.

"That was close," Aimee said, flailing with her right arm. "Wait, I'm not . . . wait . . ."

Madison wanted to let go, but her glove got

stuck somehow in the crook of Aimee's arm. She tried very hard not to cross her right ski over her left ski and lose her balance, but—

Crash.

The two friends fell on top of each other.

Everyone in the group started to laugh.

Madison and Aimee were a twisted clump of skis, poles, and snow. Carlos ran over to untangle them.

"Well, that was graceful," Aimee said, as Carlos helped her to her feet.

"It happens to everyone," Carlos said, loud enough for the rest of the group to hear. "This is why we must be so careful on the slopes. Yes?"

"I don't understand why we have to do all these exercises," Aimee said. "Wouldn't it just be easier to ski down a hill?"

Carlos shook his head. "Oh, no," he said. "You must practice before you become the safe skier."

He helped Madison to her feet, too. "You okay?" Carlos asked.

Madison nodded, even though her face, which had been pushed into the snow, felt like a slushy drink from Freeze Palace back home. She was happy to be wearing the toasty new ski pants that Stephanie had bought for her.

Hugh came over. "Are you two okay?" he asked Madison and Aimee. "I wish I had caught that one on video."

Aimee shrugged. "We're fine, I guess, if

embarrassing yourself completely is considered okay. I mean, look at us. We look like snowballs. . . ."

Madison grinned. "We really are fine," she said sweetly.

"I think we should just ski down the hill," Aimee said, looking off into the distance. "Aren't those your friends over there?" she asked.

Hugh glanced over to where Aimee was pointing. On a small slope off to the side, his three friends were lining up and trying out new moves on their skis.

"Yeah, those are my friends, but they're really, really good skiers," Hugh said. "Wick has been skiing since he was three or something."

"How hard can it be to do what they're doing?" Aimee asked. "I'm a dancer. I bet I could do that."

Madison nudged Aimee and Hugh. "We'd better go line up. Carlos wants us over there."

"Attention, everyone!" Carlos called.

The lesson was half over for the day. Carlos gathered everyone together and explained about a special Peeweeski and Teenski demonstration for parents. The instructors wanted to join together and host the presentation in a few days. Everyone in Teenski would ski with a partner.

"It's a very, very good way to practice if you have a ski buddy. Everyone stays a lot safer. It really helps when we start using the ski lift," Carlos said. "So, here's what we do."

He pointed to every other person lined up in front of him.

"Turn to the person on your right. He or she will be your lucky partner," Carlos said.

Aimee gasped. She was standing to the right of Beth, not Madison.

But Madison grinned. Hugh was on her right.

So, Hugh is Mr. Right, after all, Madison thought, her stomach flip-flopping as it always did. Her mind raced with thoughts of participating in the demo and getting a giant round of applause from all of the spectators. After that, Hugh would tell Madison that she was the best skier he had ever met. Then he would say how much he wished he could see her again—back home in Far Hills. He would ask Madison for her phone number or at least her e-mail address and then . . .

"Maddie," Aimee elbowed Madison in the side. "Why didn't you ask to switch partners?"

Madison looked over at Hugh. "I don't know," she said, even though she knew very well why she'd stuck with Mr. Right.

Aimee was red in the face. At first, Madison wasn't sure if it was the wet and cold or if Aimee was truly upset. Then she knew. Aimee turned around on her skis and moved away.

"I guess I'll go find my other partner, then," Aimee said, sounding disappointed. She slid slowly over toward Carlos, who was speaking to Beth and another pair of skiers.

"Your friend looks bummed," Hugh said. "You should ski with her."

"I do everything with her," Madison blurted. "I would rather ski with you." Had she really just said that? She almost felt as if she were baring her soul—and perhaps betraying her friend, just a little. But she stuck with Hugh.

They wobbled around on their skis a bit, practicing the wedge and trying to ski short distances on one ski for balance. They talked about school, home, and pets. Hugh owned Trix, the cat that was staying with the hotel pet-sitter.

Carlos made the rounds, checking in on his beginning skiers as everyone practiced and fell down and practiced and fell down some more.

After about fifteen minutes, Madison heard Carlos yell.

"No! No!" he cried. "Stop!"

Carlos started to chase after something—or someone—Madison couldn't tell. All of the kids in the lesson group slid after him. Madison and Hugh slid along, too.

Madison craned her neck to see what was going on.

Hugh saw right away. "It's your friend," he said. "She's skiing on the other slope."

"What?" she cried. But then she saw, too. Aimee had skipped over to the other slope. She was at the top of a fairly steep incline. A cluster of younger kids were skiing the same minislope.

Aimee didn't turn around, even though she must have heard Carlos calling after her. Didn't she hear the rest of the Teenski group yelling, "Stop! Stop!"?

Obviously not.

Instead of stopping, Aimee leaned into her skis like a real pro skier and started down the slope. Right after she'd begun, she picked up a lot of speed, and she narrowly missed colliding with a little boy in a yellow jacket; then she veered off to the side, and . . .

Madison's eyes grew wide as she watched her friend skid into a turn and tumble down a few yards, skis flying into the air along with a flurry of powder. It looked like an outtake from *Funny Home Videos*, a cable TV show. Only no one was laughing.

Aimee didn't seem to be moving.

The other little kids who had been skiing around the same area scooted over to see what had happened. Carlos got there at about the same time.

"Aimee!" Carlos cried as he removed his own skis and knelt down by her side. "Don't move, okay?"

Madison and Hugh made their way over to the scene of the accident.

Aimee's eyes were open, but she wasn't moving.

Madison's heart was thumping. She almost slammed into someone herself as she moved to get closer to her BFF.

"Aimee?" Madison said. "Aimee, say something."

By then, the Big Mountain ski patrol had been informed of the accident. A man and woman, both wearing black-and-red parkas, came over with a transport toboggan. Everyone else was ordered to move out of the way.

"Where are they taking her?" Madison asked.

"They will take Aimee to the bottom of the hill and get her to a doctor," Carlos explained.

Madison's words caught in her throat. She choked back a sob. "Oh, my . . . no . . . this can't be happening. Aimee!"

The ski patrollers leaned in closer to Aimee and started to get her ready for the descent.

"She'll be okay," Hugh said. "It didn't look like too bad a fall."

But Madison didn't really hear what Hugh was saying. She didn't hear any of the commotion around her on the hill, either.

All Madison knew was that she was staring at Aimee right now.

And her best friend wouldn't even look at her.

This was the worst kind of luck *ever*.

Chapter 10

The ski patrol loaded Aimee onto the toboggan while everyone stood whispering and pointing.

By now, a small crowd of people other than the Teenski group had gathered to watch what was going on. It reminded Madison of a highly charged episode of some TV drama. She half expected a chopper to swoop down out of the sky or some SWAT team to take position.

Carlos paced in the snow.

"I have to tell my dad and stepmom what happened," Madison said to Carlos. "I want to talk to Aimee."

"We are now trying to get in touch with your parents," Carlos explained. "Whenever there is a medical emergency, you find the adult who signed the permission form. She'll be fine. Don't worry."

Don't worry? It was too late for that.

Carlos led Madison over to Peter, a member of the ski patrol who'd just arrived on a snowmobile. He told Madison to put on a helmet and climb aboard. Peter would take Madison down the mountain and deliver her to her parents and Aimee. There, doctors would examine Aimee and then take her to the hospital emergency room if she had any serious injuries.

Madison waved a solemn good-bye to Hugh, tugged the silver helmet on over her ski hat, and climbed on to the snowmobile. Now it really did feel like a scene from a movie.

"Hold on!" Peter said in a gruff voice. Madison closed her eyes and imagined every action-movie hero she'd ever loved revving up a motorcycle or powering up a speedboat. She was off in the pursuit of danger . . . hot on the trail of a sinister spy . . . ready for anything. . . .

Whooooooooa!

The snowmobile lurched a little, and Madison snapped back to reality. She wrapped her arms around Peter's midsection and clung to him as the snowmobile slowly (not at movie-style, break-neck speed) wove past obstacles and down the mountain.

Although they were driving toward Aimee,

Madison's thoughts began to drift even more as they motored along. The air felt colder than cold; yet the sun was stronger and hotter than ever. Wind pounded her from all sides. Everything they passed was a blur of snow and color.

Peter stopped the snowmobile near an unmarked low stone building. Inside were a few of Big Mountain's medical personnel.

By the time Madison had wandered inside, Aimee had already been placed on the examining table. Madison caught her breath when she saw her BFF lying there as still a mummy.

But then Aimee's eyes moved. They locked onto Madison's.

"What happened?" Aimee asked weakly. "I feel so dizzy."

A doctor leaned over and shone a penlight into Aimee's eyes. "Well, my dear," the doctor said. "You have a slight concussion, and I'm afraid you may have a broken bone—or maybe just a sprain. We'll need to shoot you over to the hospital for a few X-rays and tests."

Aimee frowned. "Broken bone? Where? I can't have anything broken. . . ." her voice trailed off.

Madison approached the table and leaned into Aimee as much as she could. "I'm so glad you're all right," Madison whispered.

Aimee's face scrunched up. Her eyes filled with tears. "Oh, Maddie, I'm scared. What's happening?"

"You fell on the mountain," Madison said. "You skied away from the group, and you fell."

"I don't remember," Aimee said. She choked on the words. "Oh, I do remember now. I wanted to ski for real. I thought it would be easy. . . ."

The doctor came back over to Aimee and wrapped a blood-pressure cuff around her arm.

"Blood pressure is a little low," the doctor said. "But that's okay. We'll get you a place to rest so you can be calm before some of the other tests. And I might get you an IV drip, just to make sure you're hydrated."

Madison was shaking. It all felt so serious, being in this room with a real doctor and the big, hulking ski patroller. She wished she could think of something to make Aimee feel better.

"Maddie, don't leave me," Aimee called out. When she moved her arm, she yelled in pain. The doctor rushed over.

"You need to keep still," he warned Aimee. "I am pretty sure you sprained your wrist. But we need X-rays to make sure there are no broken bones here or anywhere else. We'll stabilize that arm as soon as possible."

Just then, Dad and Stephanie came rushing into the room.

"Aimee!" Dad cried when he saw Aimee lying on a stretcher. "What happened?"

Everyone rushed to fill Dad in on the accident.

Stephanie stood by Aimee, stroking the top of her head, trying to get her to breathe slowly and close her eyes.

They had to wait a few minutes before the ambulance came to take them all to the hospital for the tests.

"It all happened so fast, Dad. Aimee was just skiing and then—" Madison grabbed Dad's hand and squeezed. "I've never seen Aimee so scared."

"The doctor tells me she has a bad concussion from the fall. He thinks she must have conked her head on something, like a rock or maybe a piece of someone else's ski equipment. And her wrist is probably sprained. But other than that, I think she's all right. When we got the news we were headed onto a ski lift back up the mountain. We got off just in time and raced right over here."

Madison glanced over at Aimee. Her eyes were still wet with tears.

"We'll call your parents right away, Aimee," Stephanie said, always the voice of reason. She took out her cell phone.

"Can I talk to them?" Aimee mumbled.

Stephanie nodded. "Let me just tell your mom what happened, and then I will put you on the phone."

Aimee rolled her eyes and let out a huge sigh. "My dad and mom are going to spaz out when they hear about this. They told me to be extra careful, and now look at me."

Madison leaned into Aimee. "You'll be okay, Aim," she cooed.

Aimee reached for Madison's hand with her one good arm. She kept the weak wrist at her side.

"Maddie?" Aimee said in a soft voice. "What am I going to do? If I hurt myself it means I can't do that ballet performance when we get back to Far Hills. My teacher will be so disappointed. She's counting on me for two solos. I practiced all through the fall for that. What am I going to do?"

"Maybe your wrist will be fine," Madison said.

Aimee tried to move the wrist but then yelped in pain.

"I don't think so," Aimee said.

Stephanie had left the room to try contacting Aimee's parents, but neither Mr. nor Mrs. Gillespie was at home. Not one of Aimee's brothers answered the phone, either. The line at the Cyber Cafe was busy.

"Where is everyone?" Aimee moaned. She sobbed again. "Where's my mom? Where are my dumb brothers?" she asked.

Stephanie gave Aimee a kiss on the head. "Shhh," Stephanie said. "Don't get all worked up. We'll try your mom and dad when we get to the hospital, okay? They'll make you feel better."

Finally, the doctor put through official orders for Aimee to be driven to the local hospital for emergency X-rays. He predicted that she would have to get a soft cast on her wrist. Dad, Stephanie, and Madison piled into a monster truck along with a representative from Big Mountain.

The hospital was brand new, and everyone moved fast, as if they were gliding on ice skates. The floors were marble and the walls were covered with photographs of great skiers and ski trails.

Aimee's spirits seemed to lift a little bit once she got settled into a room. It was an hour before a Dr. Sangee arrived, wearing thick black glasses and a turban. He wheeled Aimee into a side room off the main corridor of the emergency area. Madison followed.

"Hello to you both," the doctor said, smiling broadly. He pressed a few X-rays up onto light boxes mounted on the side wall of the room. "So, Miss Gillespie," he said, pointing to an X-ray, "all seems clear. You see this thin line here? No problem. You see this gray spot here? No problem."

Aimee broke into a wide smile.

"But," Dr. Sangee continued, "I am afraid you have a bad sprain. We can fix this and help you with the pain, but you won't be able to use the wrist for a while."

"How long is a while?" Aimee asked.

"Four weeks, at least," Dr. Sangee said.

He quickly but gently pressed Aimee's arm in a few places, asked her a few more questions, and walked back out of the room.

"This isn't happening," Aimee said aloud. "This isn't happening to me."

"You'll be okay," Madison said.

Aimee turned away. Was she crying again?

Dr. Sangee returned with the material he needed to wrap Aimee's wrist and place a soft cast on the injury.

"When will my wrist be normal again?" Aimee asked. "I have to dance in a recital back home next week. Can't I put on a harder cast and do that?"

"Absolutely not—no activity," Doctor Sangee said. "No exceptions."

Madison could almost hear the wheels spinning in Aimee's head: sure, I'll agree to whatever you say if you just *get me out of here*. Aimee's look of terror at the words *four weeks* had now turned to a look of sadness. Madison took that as her cue. She reached for Aimee's good hand.

But Aimee pushed Madison away. "Leave me alone," she said abruptly.

Madison refused to give up that easily. She reached for the same hand again. "Aim, I just want to help you—"

"Maddie, please stop," Aimee said. "It doesn't matter what you say. This is the worst possible thing that could have happened."

There was a leather chair in a corner of the examination room. Madison walked over and collapsed into it. She could think of a few things that were worse.

"What if you had broken your leg?" Madison asked. "That would be worse than this, right? Or what if you had cut your head open or something really awful? What if you'd skied off the mountain? That would be worse."

Aimee stared off in the opposite direction. She didn't appear to be listening. Or, Madison considered, it might have been the concussion. Aimee's eyes had a glazed-over look about them.

Stephanie barged into the room. "Okay!" she announced. "I've got Mrs. Gillespie on the telephone." She handed the cell phone to Aimee. "They have rules against using these things in here, but we got permission. Go ahead and talk as long as you want."

Stephanie went over to Madison. "Why don't we give Aimee a little privacy?" she suggested.

Madison was glad to leave. Aimee wasn't really listening to her anymore, anyway. She and Stephanie went out, leaving Aimee alone in the room with the phone.

As Stephanie and Madison walked back toward the waiting area, Madison spotted Dad reading a newspaper.

"How is she?" Dad asked Madison.

Madison shrugged. "Grouchy," she said. "I was trying to be nice, but she didn't really want my help."

"Oh, honey," Dad said in a comforting voice.

"She wants your help. Aimee is just overwhelmed right now."

"What are we going to do?" Madison asked.

Dad looked at Stephanie.

Stephanie looked at Dad.

"I think we probably should head back to Far Hills," Stephanie said.

Dad concurred. "Aimee's parents are worried. They know she's in good hands, but they want to see her for themselves."

"Go back to Far Hills?" Madison asked. "You mean end the winter vacation? *Now?*"

Stephanie nodded. "It seems like the smart thing to do."

"No, it doesn't!" Madison blurted out. "Why do we have to go back? Why can't her parents come and pick her up?"

"Maddie . . ." Stephanie said, trying to calm her down.

"I can't believe this is happening!" Madison said.

Dad scratched his head. "I had a feeling you might see it this way," he said. "But I know you understand why we have to do it this way, Maddie. Stephanie and I are just as disappointed as you are."

A picture of Hugh flashed into Madison's mind.

"No way! You are definitely *not* as upset as I am!" Madison said.

Dr. Sangee was on his way back in to Aimee's room, but he stopped to talk to Dad. "So," he said.

"We have the release papers here. Aimee should be fine. Have her doctor call me with any questions when she returns home. I think the biggest thing you need to watch for is any possible complications from her concussion. It wasn't too bad, though. Keep her hydrated and happy."

Dad and Stephanie thanked the doctor for his help. They signed the release papers, and, once they'd picked up Aimee, the four left the hospital. They boarded a shuttle bus headed back to Treetops.

The ride was mostly silent. Neither Aimee nor Madison talked at all. Madison gazed out the window. As they left the downtown area where the hospital was situated, traffic picked up. Enormous pine trees rose up like giants, casting shadows over wide tracts of ground. A huge cloud darkened one side of the mountain.

"Aimee?" Stephanie asked. "Did you and your mother discuss our heading back to Far Hills?"

Aimee nodded without saying a word, which seemed to make Stephanie a little nervous.

"Aimee? Are you still feeling dizzy?" Stephanie asked.

"She looks fine to me," Madison said.

Aimee shot her a look. "Yeah. I'm fine. I just fell down a mountain."

"Sorry," Madison grumbled.

"Girls," Dad cautioned from the front seat. "Let's be nice, shall we? We'll head back to the chalet, have a nice supper, a good sleep, and we'll hit the road in the morning."

Madison wanted to scream. She hated the idea of leaving when it seemed as if the fun had only just begun. She'd been so panicked about clothes and skis and boys, and now . . . things were just starting to look up.

"Did you cancel our lessons and everything?" Madison asked.

Dad shook his head. "Oh, no, I haven't canceled a thing yet. We'll take care of all that in the morning."

Madison settled back in her seat.

Maybe Aimee's wrist would heal overnight and everything could go right back to normal, she thought. Maybe the vacation wouldn't be called to a screeching halt. Maybe Madison would get another chance to hang out with Hugh.

She glanced over at Aimee, curled up in her own seat in the car. Aimee's eyes still looked a little glazed over. Deep down, Madison was worried. Her BFF had gotten hurt. That was serious. How could Madison think about herself at a time like this? Suddenly she felt ashamed for wanting to stay.

They pulled into Treetops and headed for their chalet. Dad got a ride back to the mountain to pick Phinnie up. Stephanie stayed with the girls and made arrangements to have room service deliver dinner.

Aimee said her head was pounding, so Stephanie made her go and lie down. Then Stephanie lit a fire.

"Do you need help?" Madison asked halfheartedly before she plopped down onto an overstuffed couch in the living room.

Stephanie shook her head. "No, you just relax. I'll call and order the food. It's been a crazy day."

Stephanie's cell phone was sitting on the table next to the couch. Madison picked it up and dialed.

"Mom?" Madison whispered when her mother answered. "I'm so glad you're home!"

"I was just thinking of you!" Mom said.

"You were?"

"I was thinking that you must be quite the ski bunny," Mom said.

"Mom, I miss you," Madison said.

"Uh-oh. What's wrong?" Mom asked.

"Why do you think something is wrong?" Madison asked.

"I can tell."

Madison sighed. "Aimee hurt her wrist. We just got back from the hospital."

"Is she all right? What hospital? Where?" Mom fired questions at her.

"No, don't worry. She's okay now; it's just a sprain, but we had to go to the emergency room and now Dad's probably going to call off the vacation and I am really bummed," Madison replied.

"Well, I'm sorry you're bummed—but I'm glad Aimee is okay," Mom said. "Has the trip been fun so far—until today's accident, that is?"

"Not exactly," Madison said. "Aimee and I have been fighting a lot."

"Fighting about what?" Mom asked.

"I don't know. Look, I don't feel like talking about it," Madison said.

"Honey bear, you're the one who brought it up."

"I know, but can't we talk about something else?" Madison asked.

"Will you be coming home now?" Mom asked. "I assume the Gillespies know what happened."

"Yes," Madison said. "Stephanie called them from the hospital."

The silence lingered between them on the phone line.

"Maddie? Are you okay? I love you," Mom said. She took a breath and added, "I love you more than ice cream and stars and the big old white moon." It was something Mom had used to say when Madison was a little girl.

"I love you, too, Mom," Madison replied, feeling herself get a little choked up. "I'll call tomorrow, when Dad decides what we're doing next, okay?"

"Okay."

They said their good-byes, and Madison settled back into the comfortable couch again. She closed her eyes. Aimee must have fallen asleep, she guessed, hearing silence from the bedroom. Stephanie and Dad's room was quiet, too.

Madison tried to lull herself into a nap, but she couldn't. Her eyes kept opening to scan the room. The fireplace gave off a lot of heat, and the sound of crackling wood and flames was comforting. A row of old books lined the stone mantelpiece. Madison had not noticed them before.

Out of the corner of her eye, she caught sight of something glimmering on the carpet. A quarter? A paper clip? What was it?

Madison stood up and went to look.

Her lucky ski-bunny charm! She'd left it behind that morning. She guessed that Phin must have grabbed it or that it had stuck to a scarf or sweater and traveled out into the main room. Whatever the case, Madison knew in an instant why the day on the slopes had turned into a disaster.

It was her luck to lose, and she'd lost it.

Was there any way to get her luck back again?

Chapter 11

Just as the sun was rising, Madison came out of the bedroom and sat down on the sofa, staring at the fireplace. There were nothing but ashes and charred pieces of wood there this morning. Dad and Stephanie were still in their room. Aimee was asleep, snoring as usual. Madison took that as a sign that Aimee was getting back to normal.

Madison powered up her laptop and opened her e-mailbox. A few important messages were waiting.

	FROM	SUBJECT
✉	FF_Budgefilms	HUGS
✉	GoGramma	Vacation
✉	Wetwinz	Chet is a GEEK

Mom's message was first. She'd marked her e-mail with a little red exclamation point for URGENT.

From: Fran_Budgefilms
To: MadFinn
Subject: HUGS
Date: Tues 2 Mar 7:04 AM

Honey bear, after we spoke last night I hope you felt better. Aimee probably could use a friend right now if she's missing home, and you're the best kind of best friend. I know I think so. You're my special girl.

I love you,

Mom

P.S.: I attached a picture I found in my desk. Share it with Aimee. Hugs and kisses.

<<Attachment: SnowgirlsGradeOne.jpg>>

Attached to Mom's e-mail was a photograph taken many years before. In the photo, Madison and Aimee stood in front of a huge pile of snow in the Finns' backyard. They were bundled up in funny-looking neon-colored parkas, scarves, and hats with big pom-poms on top. They almost looked as if they were joined at the hip, they clung together so closely.

It wasn't hard to remember the day the photo had been taken. The temperature had dropped to about ten degrees in Far Hills a few days after a mega-snowfall. Aimee and Madison built their very own igloo in Madison's backyard.

Madison sighed, thinking back to that day in first grade, when the photo was taken.

Then she remembered that Ivy had been there, too.

Way back before their huge third-grade fight, Ivy had been friends with both Aimee and Madison. In fact, Ivy had helped with the igloo's construction.

Madison couldn't remember why Ivy wasn't in the photograph with them. It seemed funny to think about how things had changed so much, how Ivy really had—literally—fallen out of the picture. That long-ago day in the snow seemed like a fragment of a dream, as if maybe it had never really happened.

Madison saved the photo to one of her files. She would print out a color copy for Aimee when they returned home again.

The next e-mail was a hello note from Gramma Helen. She was "up to her earlobes" in snow in Chicago, she wrote. She'd heard from Mom that Madison had gone skiing with Dad and Stephanie. "Don't fall off the mountain!" Gramma said in her note. Madison knew Gramma was kidding, of course, but she hit REPLY and told her all about Aimee's accident.

After answering Gramma's e-mail, Madison opened a note from Fiona. It had some surprising news inside.

From: Wetwinz
To: MadFinn
Subject: Chet is a GEEK
Date: Tues 2 Mar 8:31 AM

I am up and it is 5 in the morning can u believe it?!! My bed is too hard and the shades let in too much light so the minute the sun comes up it's like BLAM! I'm up too.

Chet sprained his foot! 2 bad he didn't have ur GLC! We have only been here a day. Because of him we couldn't go to the beach yesterday (it was kind of gloomy outside n e way). I am actually kind of bored. Chet is SOOOOOO mad. He called the other guys on the hockey team and I think I heard him whining to my mom. What a geek. I bet u guys r having the BEST time. I wish I were skiing 2.

Say hi to Aim 4 me.

BTW: I got an e-mail from Egg
yesterday. He said that he & Hart
went sk8ing with Drew and his gf
Emily--and Hart was talking about
YOU!!!! Isn't that GREAT? Egg thinks
that Hart is going to ask u out on
a real date when we get back home.
I know he's said it b4 but maybe
this time it's 4 real? I hope so. I
think u should 4get finding a new
crush at Big Mountain. You haven't
met someone u like more yet, have
u? Well, DON'T!!!!! WBS.

xoxoxoxoxxo

Big smoochies,

Fiona

Madison instantly hit REPLY.
She wanted to tell Fiona about Hugh—and
about Aimee's fall on the mountain, too. But
as she typed, Madison realized that she couldn't
write about Hugh. She couldn't put the whammy on
a new relationship by *talking about it*. Talking about
things too much brought the worst luck, didn't it?
DELETE.
Madison yawned. She was overthinking things
again. Why was she even worried about Hugh

when he was practically ancient history? There would be no more cute ski partner. No more Treetops or Big Mountain. Dad had made it perfectly clear: they were heading home today. The coolest winter break in the history of Madison Finn's life was ending.

And that was that.

Madison opened a new file and started to type.

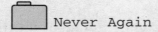 Never Again

Dad came back with Phinnie and he's curled up in my lap right now. Thank goodness he's here. I feel better than I did an hour ago, but that's not saying much.

I wonder how Aimee feels? She's been crashing out in the bedroom for a while now. I feel so bad about the fact that she hurt herself. But I'm also kind of upset because now our vacation is ruined. I knew it had to be too good to be true. And I told Aimee she should wear her bunny charm. Why didn't she listen to me?

Rude Awakening: I thought that coming on this ski trip made me the luckiest duck. As it turns out, Big Mountain is not all it's quacked up to be. LOL.

I guess I can live if I don't see Hugh again even though I sincerely thought we made some kind of real connection. Okay, I only knew him for two days, but still.

And--big surprise--I still don't know
how I feel about Hart. He chased me around
in third grade and I was like, "cooties!"
so he and I never had instant sparks like
I did w/Hugh on the slopes the other day.
Hart's more like one of these guys who
starts as a real good friend and should
probably just stay that way esp. since
he calls me Finnster. I mean that is just
about the most UN-romantic name in the

"Maddie, can I talk to you?" Aimee shuffled
across the floor in a pair of bunny slippers that she'd
brought along for the trip.

"Hey, Aim," Madison said, hitting a quick SAVE
and pressing the button that made the white rhi-
noceros screen saver appear on Madison's computer
screen. "How are you feeling?"

Aimee sat on the comfy sofa next to Madison and
crossed her hands neatly in her lap. Madison stared
at the cast on Aimee's wrist.

"Does it hurt?" Madison asked.

Aimee shook her head. "Only when I breathe,"
she said dramatically.

Madison laughed. "I'm really sorry that you fell,"
she said.

"Why are you sorry?" Aimee said. "I'm the one
who fell."

"Oh," Madison said. "I just meant . . . well . . . I
feel bad."

"Why?" Aimee asked. "Don't feel bad."

"Well, I feel bad that you won't be able to ski in the presentation or finish the lessons."

"Oh, no. I'll be there," Aimee said. "We'll both be there."

Madison did a double take. "What?" she said. "Aim, the doctor said you should rest. And Dad said we'd be going home this morning."

"No, we're not," Aimee said. "Yesterday my parents said I could stay if I wanted. I just wasn't sure."

"We're staying? *Really?*" Madison asked.

Aimee nodded. "I hope that's okay. . . . I just have to tell your dad. . . ."

"What do you mean, 'if it's okay'?" Madison cried. A wide grin spread across her face, and she lurched forward to give Aimee a bear hug. Of course, she stumbled while doing it, nearly squashing Aimee's cast, and stubbing her own toe at the same time, but it didn't matter.

They were staying.

Madison dashed into the next room, waving her arms. "Stephanie! Dad! Aimee has something to tell us. It's very important. She's staying!"

Phinnie got excited by all the commotion. He jumped on and off the sofa at least five or six times, panting wildly.

"What did you say?" Stephanie asked. "You're hungry?

"No, no, no, no, *no*! Aimee's staying," Madison cried. She could hardly form a complete sentence—she was *that* excited.

"Is this true, Aimee?" Dad asked. "You want to stay?"

Aimee nodded. "Yes," she said. "I thought about it a lot. I just don't want to ruin anyone's vacation—not even my own. And if I go back I'll just have to work in my dad's store even with my sprained wrist, so I'd rather hang out at a cool chalet and watch Madison put everyone else into the deep freeze at the ski presentations this week. Is that okay?"

"If that's what you want, Aimee," Madison's dad said. "I'll call your parents and let them know."

The next morning, Aimee helped Madison get ready for their sunny day on the slopes. Even with a cast on, Aimee was a fashion expert. She looked good, too, Madison noticed. With or without injuries, Aimee looked like a ski catalog model, all dressed up in her navy ski pants and the flowered wool sweater she'd been bragging about.

"Why are you so dressed up?" Madison asked.

Aimee shrugged. She pulled out a tube of eyeliner.

"Hey, you don't even wear makeup!" Madison said.

"Yes, I do . . . sometimes," Aimee said. "I just don't talk about it. "And you know, my mom says that most cosmetic companies test their products on animals, so I'm not allowed to touch mascara or even lip gloss unless it's a cruelty-free product."

Aimee stared at herself intently in the mirror. It was hard to apply eyeliner with only one free hand.

"Can I wear some?" Madison asked, looking at herself in the mirror, too.

Aimee leaned in and applied a little eyeliner to Madison's lids. Madison blinked. She looked different with makeup. Maybe Hugh would notice her more. After her minimakeover, Madison dressed in her ski pants and other layers, including her oversize Far Hills sweatshirt, a lavender Henley shirt, and a pale blue scarf she'd borrowed from Mom. Then she hooked her ski-bunny chain and charm around her neck like a KEEP OUT BAD LUCK sign. She wasn't taking any chances today. No way.

"Wow! Maddie!" Aimee said. She stood back and put her fingers up in front of her eyes as if she were a fake photographer taking a picture. "You look . . ."

Snap. Snap. Snap.

"FAB-ulous . . ."

Snap. Snap. Snap.

Madison posed like a starlet, going along with Aimee's compliments and the pretend photography session. Then she broke into a small fit of giggles.

"I started this trip as a fashion disaster, and now I'm ready to walk the runway!" Madison said, still cracking up.

"Maybe we'll see Foster Lane again," Aimee said. "And he'll give you a part in his next big movie!"

Madison was glad to be laughing again.

"What is so funny?" Stephanie asked, walking into the room. "Are you girls getting ready or preparing a comedy routine?"

Dad walked inside, hands crossed like he was thinking really hard.

"You're sure you feel comfortable heading up to the mountain, Aimee?" he asked. "Because we can stay together here and go shopping or something else if you want. Madison probably won't miss the ski lessons; will you, Maddie?"

Madison wanted to scream. Of course she would miss the lessons, Dad! She had to go to the lessons, Dad! It was all about *the lessons*, Dad!

Aimee was the one who answered. "No, I want to go up the mountain, Mr. Finn," she said sweetly. "I think Maddie wants to do that ski demo they're having this week. I can probably help the instructor keep score or something. Right, Maddie?"

Madison smiled to herself. The old Aimee was back! Of course she knew Aimee had another, ulterior motive for staying: she wanted to see Carlos again (even if she'd never admit it).

The four of them boarded the shuttle to Big Mountain with Phin in tow. Aimee volunteered to babysit him while Madison skied, but the resort regulations didn't allow pets in the main lodge or on the slopes. So he was sent off to spend his day with the other animals, including Trix, Hugh's cat.

Carlos was relieved to see Aimee returning to the class—and was impressed that she was willing to assist with scorekeeping and other tasks. But mostly, Carlos just had Aimee sit around like a cheerleader. Aimee didn't seem to mind. Even off the slopes she could still find a way to get all the attention she needed.

Meanwhile, Madison and Hugh went to work, practicing their basic ski exercises together like synchronized swimmers—poles extended, skis wedged, the works. As midafternoon approached, they prepared to learn the hardest lesson of all: how to get on to the ski lift.

"I'm going to fall on my butt again," Madison said.

"Nah. You can't mess this up," Hugh said.

For a moment, Madison feared the snow all around her would melt into an enormous puddle. She didn't know what to say back to Hugh.

Every spot on Big Mountain had its own special name, including the ski lifts. One was called To the Top. Another one was named Take a Peak. But the ski lift that Carlos wanted the group to practice on was called Four-Leaf Clover. Naturally, Madison saw that as a very, *very* lucky omen.

Carlos lined the group up and explained how to

board the lift. He made it sound easy, but Madison wasn't so sure.

"First, remove the pole straps from your wrists," Carlos explained. "Then proceed to the point before the lift loading area. Stop at the line marking the point before the lift that's in the snow. Wait for a chair to swing past. You should be at the line marking the loading area. Now, stop there and place both poles in your inside hand. Watch for the next chair coming toward you. Grab the seat pole for balance and take the seat."

"And don't fall," Hugh muttered under his breath.

"Yes, don't fall!" Carlos said. "That would be a bad thing. Right, Miss Aimee?"

Aimee rolled her eyes. "Yes, Carlos," she said, bowing her head. Aimee hardly ever got embarrassed, but she was close to being embarrassed then.

A few in the group laughed.

Madison raised her hand to ask a question.

"What happens to our skis?" Madison asked. "Do we keep them on? I mean, I can see everyone on the lift has their skis on, but . . ."

"Ah, yes!" Carlos nodded. "The skis! Keep your skis separated, with the tips up, as you glide forward and are lifted off the ground. And don't forget to look down. You'll have an incredible view once you are in the air."

Madison gazed up into the sky and watched the

other skiers making their way back up the mountain on the lift. The view must have been great, just as Carlos had said.

Of course, the view here, next to Hugh, wasn't so bad, either.

Chapter 12

Madison and Aimee sat around the living-room fire-place. Phin was there, too, chewing on a rawhide toy, looking up occasionally to check out the fire and sigh one of his little doggy sighs.

They were alone, just the three of them. Dad and Stephanie had gone to a complimentary cocktail party in the Treetops restaurant—for adults only. Although they weren't sure about going out, Dad and Stephanie decided at the last minute to go. It wasn't as if the restaurant were very far. It was just a five-minute walk from the room.

Since their return that afternoon from skiing, Madison and Aimee had watched an extreme sports special on the skiing channel, hosted by none other than their favorite superstar, Foster Lane. They'd eaten thin mints and half a bag of corn chips, *and* they'd drunk root beer (Madison was glad her favorite soda was stocked in the kitchenette fridge).

The chalet was quieter than quiet, except for the occasional sound of the wind coming in at the many windows and skylights and the crackling fire, of course. A few times Madison jumped, convinced that she heard voices or footsteps or loud thunks that she was sure had to be Mr. White, the ghost the waiter had told them about on their first night in the resort.

Madison taught Aimee how to play crazy eights just the way Gramma Helen played it. They fed Phinnie his kibble. Eventually, the laptop came out and they started surfing around. Their first stop was the bigfishbowl.com Web site. Madison and Aimee headed for the fortune-telling area called Ask the Blowfish.

"Will Ben Buckley become Aimee's one true love?" Madison asked the blowfish.

"What kind of a question is *that*?" Aimee said, whacking Madison's shoulder with her one good arm. "I don't like Ben *that* much. And I don't believe that a computer can tell me who my one true love is."

Madison rolled her eyes. "Okay. I change my question to: 'Will Carlos the ski instructor become Aimee's one true love?'"

"*Maddie!*" Aimee shrieked, pretending to be shocked by the new question. "Cut it out!"

The blowfish's answer to Madison's question came up in an underwater bubble: "Outlook not clear. Ask again."

Aimee hit the ESCAPE key on the laptop. "I'm bored. Let's play something else," she suggested. But before they could decide what else to do, an Insta-Message box popped up in the corner of the screen.

<Wetwinz>: R U there????

In unison, Aimee and Madison let out a shrill cry that caused Phin to drop his chew toy and dash into the next room.

"I'm not bored anymore!" Aimee said, diving for the keyboard.

Madison typed the first response.

<MadFinn>: HELLOOOOOOOOOOOO!
    ((Fiona)):**
<Wetwinz>: I took a chance that u
    guys would be home @ nite maybe
    watching TV or going online I am
    soooo lucky to find u guys OMG
    how is UR wrist aim??? I got
    Maddie's email and I was SOOOO
    worried
<MadFinn>: it's ok Aimee can't ski
    but we stayed n e way at the
    resort
<Wetwinz>: Phew (that ur ok) chet is

146

```
      ok 2 I think I told u he
      busted up his ankle it was
      actually just a sprain too but he
      can't do ANYTHING
<MadFinn>: bummer
<Wetwinz>: I can do stuff though &
      I went to my 1st surfing lesson
<MadFinn>: KOOL
<Wetwinz>: I didn't exactly go in
      the water yet
<MadFinn>: I didn't exactly ski down
      a mountain yet
<Wetwinz>: so what's the status on
      the crush? Spill it
```

Aimee pushed Madison away from the keyboard. "Maddie, you won't tell her the truth. Let me type." Madison watched Aimee respond.

```
<MadFinn>: ok it's me Aim--Maddie is
      IN LOVE with this guy Hugh and he
      actually lives close to home
<Wetwinz>: wow T^
<MadFinn>: He is cuter than Hart
      even
<Wetwinz>: wow sounds serious
<MadFinn>: did Maddie tell u that we
      saw Foster Lane?
<Wetwinz>: R U KIDDING ME? Foster
      Lane is a hottie.
```

147

\<MadFinn\>: He asked us to be in one
    of his movies J/J
\<Wetwinz\>: LOL look we're not going
    back to Far Hills until Sunday so
    I won't see you until school
\<MadFinn\>: :>(
\<Wetwinz\>: BTW did u get an e-mail
    from Lindsay?
\<MadFinn\>: no Y?
\<Wetwinz\>: I think our chain letter
    worked!
\<MadFinn\>: huh?
\<Wetwinz\>: Lindsay saw Ivy Daly in
    downtown yesterday and she was
    wearing a hat pulled down around
    her head
\<MadFinn\>: SW? It's cold out
    everyone wears hats
\<Wetwinz\>: NONONONONONONO something
    was up with her hair Lindsay
    said she heard a rumor that
    Ivy's hair got gum in it or
    something and she had to cut
    it short.
\<MadFinn\>: well that's good news
\<Wetwinz\>: AND good luck 2 :>)
\<MadFinn\>: It def. had 2 be the
    chain letter I told u and Aimee
    those things really work.
\<Wetwinz\>: BTW thanks for the
    digital pic maddie I loved it

148

```
<MadFinn>: I loved it 2--Aim posing
   on the slopes!
<Wetwinz>: in a pile of snow LOL
MadFinn>: we both miss u so much
Wetwinz>: next time we have a school
   break--let's NOT break us up, ok?
<MadFinn>: :>)
<Wetwinz>: GG--send me another
   e-mail tomorrow if u can and
   more pictures PLEEZ
```

Madison logged off. Aimee lounged on the sofa, her feet up.

"Maddie?" Aimee said softly, scratching Phin's ears. The pug had padded back into the room and was now stretched out on top of Aimee's stomach. "Maybe you're right."

Madison flopped onto another chair. "Right about what?" she asked Aimee.

"I don't know," Aimee said. "Right about all this good-luck stuff. I mean, it makes sense. We left the chain letter in Ivy's locker, and see what happened?"

"Right," Madison said, nodding. "And you didn't wear your bunny charm, and see what happened to you?"

Aimee glanced down at her wrist. "I was just showing off, you know."

"What do you mean?" Madison said.

"I was showing off," Aimee admitted again.

"And then when it happened, I was way too embarrassed to even talk about it. I felt like the biggest moron on the planet. Usually when I have a tough variation or a hard step in ballet, I stick it on the first try. But skiing was harder for me."

"It's okay," Madison said.

"No, it's not," Aimee said, "I almost messed up our entire vacation—including for your dad and Stephanie, too, because I was being dumb."

"I was being dumb, too," Madison said. She paused. "I'm sorry."

"I'm sorry, too!" Aimee declared.

Madison and Aimee both reached out for a hug at the same time.

"I have something to show you," Madison said once they'd already embraced. Madison clicked around on her laptop until the photo Mom had sent filled the screen.

"That's *us*!" Aimee said when she saw the picture.

"We'll be friends forever, " Madison said.

"Friends forever," Aimee agreed.

The Big Ski area of the ski slopes seemed unusually crowded that morning. Of course, numerous families were hanging out today for the special demonstrations. Not only were different groups showing off whatever they'd learned at ski lessons, but staff members were doing snowboard and snow-tubing tricks for the gallery. Ski patrollers were also sponsoring safety talks. Dad and Stephanie walked around, talking with another couple they'd met at the party the night before.

Aimee helped Carlos prepare for the presentation by keeping everyone in a good mood. Several of the parents were buzzing about Aimee's recent accident. Apparently anyone who fell on Big Mountain turned into a momentary mountain celebrity.

Carlos asked partners to pair up and practice. The technique demonstration would begin after a few run-throughs.

Madison spotted Hugh hanging around at the side of the slope with his crew of spectators: Philip, Wick, and Roger. He waved Madison over.

"Hi," Madison said. Hugh introduced her to everyone.

"I was looking for you," Hugh said.

"You were?" Madison said, with a lilt in her voice.

"Yeah, I have a slight problem," Hugh said.

"Oh, really?" Madison asked. She reached into her jacket and felt around for the end of her ski-bunny necklace and nervously played with the rabbit charm. "Um . . . what's the problem?"

"I can't ski with you today," Hugh said.

It was as if the entire mountaintop had gone silent. Madison's head whirred. She wasn't sure she'd heard him correctly.

"What did you say?" Madison asked.

"I can't ski with you. Sorry. I have to go be with

my friends and my parents," he said. "Well, I don't really see the point in this demo anyway, do you? I mean, we practiced, but it all seems kind of stupid now. . . ."

"But the ski presentation only takes half an hour," Madison said. "You can't do it at all?"

Hugh shook his head. "I'm really sorry. It was fun hanging out, though."

Madison felt herself swoon a little—but not in a good way. She took a deep breath so she wouldn't tumble into the snow on her skis. She looked right at Hugh and then over at his friends. The other boys were whispering and smiling.

Madison knew exactly what was going on. His friends had put him up to this.

"What's wrong with you?" she asked Hugh.

"What do you mean?" Hugh said. "I just told you. And I said I was sorry. I don't know what the big deal is. . . ."

Hugh's friend Wick spoke up.

"Look, Hughie can't do it. Why don't you just find another partner?" Wick said.

Madison froze.

Was this what it felt like to be buried by a sudden avalanche on a mountaintop in the middle of nowhere? Madison felt *that* alone. Plus, she was outnumbered four to one.

"I'm really, really sorry," Hugh said again.

"You're sorry?" Madison repeated.

"Maybe we can ski some other time?" Hugh asked.

It sounded as though Hugh were trying to be nice. But Madison knew better. Trying wasn't good enough. *He* wasn't good enough. Slowly, Madison got into the wedge ski position and carefully turned herself around.

"Wait. Madison?" Hugh called out after her.

Madison didn't turn around. It was taking all her concentration not to cross her skis and crash down into the snow in a hysterical, sobbing mess.

Carlos was busy making sure everyone was practicing and getting their equipment together. He had set out stereo speakers for musical accompaniment to the demonstration. Aimee helped him get those set up.

Madison made a beeline for her BFF.

Her face must have been saying, *Help me now,* because as soon as Aimee saw her, she came crunching toward her in her clunky ski boots.

"Maddie, what's wrong? Where's Hugh going?" Aimee asked.

Madison turned around and saw that Hugh had skied away with his three friends. Just like that.

"He's gone," Madison said.

"Wait, I'm confused," Aimee said. "He's *gone*? But the demo is starting soon. He's your partner."

Madison glared at Aimee. "No kidding."

"Seriously, he's coming back, isn't he?" Aimee

153

asked. But then she understood. "Oh, my God, he's really gone? Maddie!"

Madison felt like she'd been slammed on the side of the head with a snowboard. Was it possible to get a concussion from something someone *said*?

"What am I going to do? I'm . . . all . . . alone," Madison stammered. She could feel the rush of tears coming, but she fought the urge to cry.

"You are *so* not alone," Aimee reassured her.

Madison sniffled.

"I'm here," Aimee said, putting her good arm around Madison's shoulder.

Madison unzipped the top of her parka and reached under her fleece. She fumbled for a bit and then produced the bunny-charm necklace.

"What good is this thing?" Madison cried as she yanked it off and hurled it to the ground.

Instantly, Aimee dropped to her knees and fished in the snow for the necklace. She handed it back to Madison.

"What are you doing?" Aimee asked. "You can't get rid of this. It's your lucky charm."

"There's no such thing as lucky charms or superstitions or any of it. You were right, Aimee."

Aimee pulled Madison into another hug, which was a little awkward because they were both dressed in snow gear. Madison was starting to cry, and Aimee had one wrist in a cast.

Madison stared off in the direction where Hugh

had been standing. It was just hitting her. She would never, ever, *ever* see him again.

"Maddie," Aimee whispered. "Let me show you something."

"What?" Madison asked. What could Aimee possibly have to show Madison?

Aimee unzipped her own parka and opened the top of her sweater. There, on Aimee's neck, was *her* ski-bunny charm necklace.

"You wore it?" Madison asked. "But I thought—"

"I think this week you made me believe in all that good-luck stuff," Aimee said. "Besides, my ballet teacher would really be unhappy if I sprained my other wrist, so, just in case . . ."

Madison looked down at the necklace that she held clenched in her hand. Then, smiling, she looped it around her neck once again.

"Aimee, I'm so glad you're here on this trip. You're such a good friend," Madison said. "I don't know what I would do if you weren't my friend—"

"Oh, give me a break," Aimee said. "You're the one who's great. I know sometimes I can be a pain. At least, that's what my brothers always tell me."

"I'm glad you're wearing your bunny necklace, Aimee. You know, it really looks good on you."

"Yeah, I think it matches my outfit today," Aimee said with a grin. "And I think we both need a bit of good luck."

Chapter 13

 On the Road AGAIN

So our stay here at Treetops is almost done. We're headed back to Far Hills 2day.

I did really well in the demo, actually. Carlos stepped in as my partner. Aimee was really jealous--or at least she joked around that she was. But Carlos made me look like a skiing pro. I actually skied and wedged and stopped in the right place on this little hill. I made it around all five cones he put out in this baby obstacle course. Dad and Stephanie were very impressed.

And the most incredible thing happened after the demo was over--we met Foster

Lane!!! Well, we didn't actually meet him, we saw him signing autographs. And we each got one. He signed Aimee's soft cast first, but the ink started to run because it was a little wet, so he signed a piece of paper after that. Aimee says she's going to frame it when we get home. I think she'll probably build some kind of shrine. And he is SO not that cute. He had zits!

Aimee was super happy though. She said everything worked out for the best because we stuck together.

Rude Awakening: Friends are like blankets. I never thought I'd need them so much until I got left out in the cold.

Madison had to stop typing for a moment. She was thinking again about the exact moment when Hugh had ditched her on the slopes—when she had been left out in the cold for real. Even though she'd recovered and skied the demo with Carlos, it hadn't hurt any less.

She glanced out the window of the chalet, out onto the snowy exterior of the resort. Something about the icicles, the snowdrifts, the tall, tall trees— it just didn't seem as romantic as it had a few days before.

The laptop went *bling* and Madison turned back to her e-mail. Her battery was running low. She would have to remember to plug the computer in and recharge it before the long trip home.

Madison started typing in her file again.

```
    Maybe everything that happened this week
was all meant to be--the flat tires, the
snowdrift inside the living room, Aimee's
accident, getting dumped. And maybe Aimee
and I were meant to have all those annoying
fights (they were SO annoying!)
    Maybe everything happened so we could
see that the best lucky charm was with us
all along--each other.
    It's kind of cool to think that a person
can be my best lucky charm.
```

Aimee came into the main room where Madison was sitting and typing on her laptop. Phin trotted in behind her.

"Phinnie sure does love you," Madison said.

"And I love him! I can't wait to see my puppy, Blossom, though," Aimee said. "I've missed her."

Dad strolled into the room carrying a cup of hot coffee. "So, girls," he said. "We have another day ahead of us. Stephanie and I were thinking. I know we're heading back home, but why don't we spend part of our last afternoon checking out some more of the scenery?"

Madison's face lit up. "Sure," she said. "I'm going to get dressed."

Stephanie checked them out of the hotel while Dad loaded up the Jeep. They drove to the other side of Elk Lake, where there were places to rent skates and—best of all—lots of hot chocolate.

Aimee grabbed a cup and parked herself at one of the tables. It was outdoors, but it was on a patio. Stephanie decided to sit out the skating to keep company with Aimee and Phin. Madison and Dad wandered onto the frozen lake in their rented skates.

"I haven't skated much this winter," Madison said. "I'm a little wobbly. I seem to wobble at all winter sports."

"You were great yesterday," Dad said. "I was very proud of you."

"Really?" Madison said.

"Of course. I know it has been a rough week for everyone, especially you."

"What about Aimee?" Madison asked. "It's been rough for her. I mean, she's the one who got hurt."

"Yes, but all the excitement swirled around her. You had to do most of the waiting around and the helping out. I know that can be tough," Dad said. He spun on the edge of his skate blade and did a full turn.

A little way across the lake, Madison saw some boys with hockey sticks skating circles around each other. She squinted. Was Hugh over there? She couldn't tell. They were all too far away.

Dad zipped back and forth in front of Madison, who slowly skated along, pushing off more with one foot than the other. She was beginning to wobble less, though. Her arms relaxed, too.

"Go, Maddie!" Aimee cheered from the sidelines.

Madison threw her arms up into the air and then leaned forward to take a bow. Unfortunately, the tip of her skate caught on a patch of rough ice—and there was nothing to grab on to.

"Oh, no!" Madison let out a cry.

"Hold on!" Dad skated over and scooped Madison into his arms before she fell.

Madison righted herself. She gave Dad a kiss on the cheek. "Thanks, Dad," she said.

"Hooray!" Aimee cried. "Good save!"

Later, as they left Elk Lake, Madison gazed over at the hockey players again. She could see better now. Hugh wasn't there. He really was gone for good.

The ride back to Far Hills went much faster than the ride up had gone. For one thing, Dad didn't get lost. And Aimee and Madison talked almost the entire way home.

At a rest stop, Aimee and Madison got out for a snack. Aimee grabbed an apple and handed it to Madison. Then she grabbed another apple for herself.

"Okay, now we have to do this. It will tell you who your true love is," Aimee explained.

"Aimee, you are such a faker. I thought you

didn't believe in any of this stuff! You told me!"

Aimee raised her eyebrows. "I changed my mind. So, let's play."

She started twisting off her apple stem and reciting the alphabet at the same time. It took until the letter *W* for Aimee's stem to pop off.

"That's the first letter of my true love's name," Aimee said.

"Maybe it's Egg," Madison teased. Egg's real first name was Walter.

"Very funny," Aimee said. "Now, you take the stem and poke—poke—poke—poke. . . ."

The stem poked through the apple skin on the letter *D*.

"I told you!" Madison squealed. "*W*, *D*—for *Walter Diaz*!"

"Hey, I think it really poked through on letter *C*," Aimee said.

Madison frowned. "Hey! You did that on purpose!"

"Whatever. You do it," Aimee said.

Madison twisted her stem. "A, B, C, D, E, F, G, H—"

The stem popped off.

"*H* for *Hugh*," Madison said dejectedly.

"Oh, well," Aimee said. "Try poking the skin."

Madison poked and poked. She finally pierced the skin on the letter *J*.

"Hugh Jackson!" Madison wailed. "And he

dumped me! My true love dumped me!"

Aimée held out her hands to Madison. "Maddie," she said. "You have to look at things from a different angle."

"What do you mean?" Madison asked.

"Well, H. J. doesn't just stand for *Hugh Jackson*," Aimee said.

"You're right," Madison said, gulping. She held the apple stem high in the air. "It stands for *Hart Jones*."

"Duh," Aimee said. "Maybe your new crush on Hugh was just a way to lead you back to your true love."

"You mean, Hart?" Madison asked. "My true love?"

She and Aimee exploded into a laughing fit.

Dad pulled into Aimee's driveway sometime after six o'clock. Mrs. Gillespie walked out to the car to help Aimee with her bags and to say hello (and thank) Dad and Stephanie and Madison. She fussed all over Aimee, checking out her cast—and wondering why there was a giant, smudged-ink scribble on its side.

As soon as they drove down the street and pulled into the Finns' driveway, Phinnie jumped out and raced for the porch. Mom was standing there, waving hello. She threw her arms around Madison as Dad and Stephanie backed out of the driveway.

"See you for dinner Friday!" Madison called out.

Dad honked the horn and pulled away.

Mom and Madison walked inside. Mom had ordered a pizza, which was sitting on the kitchen table.

"I got pepperoni," Mom said.

Madison licked her lips. "Mmmm," she said. "We went skating earlier this afternoon and it made me so hungry!"

They ate dinner and sat around, rehashing the events of the trip. When bedtime came, Madison dragged herself upstairs, laptop in hand.

She wanted to check in with her keypal.

```
From: MadFinn
To: Bigwheels
Subject: Home Sweet Home
Date: Thurs 4 Mar 8:59 PM
Are you still sick? I hope not! I'm
back home under my own covers right
now. I am so glad to be back from
the trip. It was fun but hard, too.
Sometimes Aimee and I are so
different. But I guess BFFs don't
have to be identical twins. Mom and
Dad both say it's the different
parts that make friendships work.

I hope u don't mind but I'm
attaching two pictures to this
e-mail. The first one is me and
```

Aimee in first grade. The second one
is a picture we took on the ski
trip. As you can see, we spent a
lot of time falling in the snow!

I wanted to share it with u b/c I
think of you as one of my BFFs too.
I hope u feel the ssme. I am so
glad I met you on bigfishbowl.com.
That was REALLY lucky, wasn't it?

Yours till the hot chocolates (with
whipped cream!),

Maddie

After Madison hit SEND, her computer made a
bling noise; she thought it was just the battery running low again. But then she realized it was an Insta-
Message. She clicked on the corner of her screen.

<Sk8rboy>: Hey I'm at egg's and we
    heard u guys came back

She nearly fell off her bed. <Sk8rboy> was Hart.

<Sk8rboy>: R U There? Egg wants 2
    know if u want to go sk8 @ the
    pond tomorrow everyone will b
    there xcept F & C b/c theyre
    still in CAL

Madison could barely catch her breath, let alone type a response.

Good luck came in all shape and sizes, she realized. And maybe the apple stem had been right. Maybe H. J. was her true love.

Madison knew only one thing for sure.

Tomorrow, she would be going to skate at the pond.

And she'd be wearing her lucky ski-bunny charm around her neck.

Mad Chat Words:

&:-P	Goofy face
] - 8	Wearing sunglasses and lip gloss
-=#:-)/	Wizard and his wand
<brrrrr>	It's so cold!
TLC	Tender loving care
GTSY	Glad to see you
404	I have NO clue
GLC	Good-luck charm
J/J	Just joking
OOTB	Out of the blue
WML	Wish me luck
WAM	Wait a minute
T^	Thumbs up
((Fiona)):**	Hugs and kisses to Fiona

Madison's Computer Tip

When I knew I'd be going to this ultrafancy ski resort, I freaked. I am always fighting with the clothes in my closet. But a quick search online showed me some cool things I could bring with me on the trip. **The Internet is a great place to search for trends, fashion tips, and other ideas about what's hot—and in my case, what's not.** Aimee and Fiona are always surfing online, and they always seem to know just what to wear. I need all the help I can get!

Visit Madison at www.lauradower.com

Laura Dower is the author of more than sixty books for kids. Like Madison Finn, Laura is an only child, enjoys her laptop computer, and drinks root beer. She lives in New York with her husband and two children.

For updates on Madison Finn and more information about the author, log on to www.lauradower.com.